Signs of Spring

written and illustrated by

Patrick Quinn

Eagle Creek Publications
Prior Lake, Minnesota

Signs of Spring / Written and illustrated by Patrick J. Quinn

Summary-Deep in the north woods of Minnesota, Eddie, a twelve-year-old hearing impaired boy, learns the true meaning of home and gains first hand knowledge of his Native American Ojibwe culture from his great-grandfather.

ISBN 0-9645048-0-4

Topic areas-[1. Native American culture-Fiction. 2. Deaf-Fiction. 3. Sign language-Fiction]

Library of Congress Catalogue Card Number 94-090774

Cover Illustration by Brian Tennessen

Eagle Creek Publications
14160 Rolling Oaks Circle NE
Prior Lake, MN 55372

To my wife, Mary, my daughter, Kelly, and son, Gavin for their love and encouragement .

I would like to sincerely thank the following people, who helped me produce Signs of Spring: Margaret Wangensteen, who provided first rate knowledge of the English language, editing skill and encouragement; Keith Johnson, for generously sharing his technical skills, time and enthusiasm; Brian Tennessen, musician, sculptor and painter, who provided the beautiful artwork for the cover; Cheryl McMahon, for use of her paper on comparisons of Native American sign language and American Sign Language; Jason Gangeness for his informative tour of his native Bemidji area in northern Minnesota; Ron Maye for his own rooster story; all the students at the New Prague Public Schools, who continue to inspire me; and my parents, Joseph and Irene, for their part in shaping my thoughts.

Chapter One

From his place in the back seat, Eddie could position himself to see the rear view mirror outside his father's window. The skyline of Minneapolis was lit by the low powerful rays of the spring sunrise. This place that had been Eddie's home for his entire twelve years was sliding farther away and into the horizon.

"Doesn't anyone have a thing to say?" Eddie's mother asked. She twisted around in the front seat of their ten-year-old Chevy station wagon with the orange trailer in tow. Banking around the cloverleaf, the wagon trudged into the northbound lane of Interstate 94 heading out of the city.

Eddie's younger sister, Nina, clutching her once white Christmas bear, pursed her lips and refused to look at her mother or answer her. Leonard, the oldest, sat staring sideways from the back passenger window, listening to a tape through headphones. Eddie slouched against the door. Through narrowed, angry eyes he watched the Minneapolis skyline shrink.

It was in this city, that Eddie LaVoi had been born with a severe hearing loss. Eddie lived on Franklin Avenue, just fifteen minutes from Seward School. There he had learned to communicate. With a mix of his high powered hearing aid, the sign language of others, and reading lips, Eddie could usually figure out what others were saying to him. And with lots of very hard work with the speech therapist, Eddie had learned to speak reasonably well.

Patiently, Posie waited while her silent children struggled to ignore her. Nina was the first to break her stare and glance toward her mother. "I don't see why we have to move to Bemidji. I hate it up there."

"You've never been to the Bemidji area! It's beautiful in the north woods. How can you hate it?" Posie looked over to her husband for support.

"We've been through this a dozen times," their father, Wes, reminded them. Nina began signing for Eddie what their father said. Checking his rear view mirrors, Wes slipped over to the left lane to pass the semi with the stack of pickup trucks. "I know this is tough on you kids, but we've decided it's for the best. We've been wanting to get out of the city for a long time now. We never used to worry about you kids playing outside by yourselves or going down to the park. It's not that way anymore. A lot of kids are ending up in trouble. Too many bad apples and they're not going to spoil my bunch of kids."

2

Eddie glared out the side window when suddenly, there was a loud thud and the car shook spilling Posie's coffee. "What was that?" called Wes as he stepped on the brake.

Twisting to his left, Eddie saw it shoot by. It rolled past going sixty and no one was steering it. "It's a wheel!" shouted Eddie. "A wheel just went by!" Eddie strained against his seatbelt and pointed.

"I think it's one of our trailer tires," said Posie, her eyes large with surprise. Wes pulled over to the side of the road and the LaVois all watched helplessly as the tire flew down the passing lane of the freeway. It edged its way toward the grassy median.

"Oh yikes," pleaded Wes watching with gritted teeth, "don't go into the oncoming traffic."

"I knew we shouldn't be moving," exclaimed Eddie. "See? Look what happens. We're hardly even out of town and the wheels are falling off! It's a bad sign."

"Like an omen?" Nina asked. "Dad is that right? An omen? Are we seeing an omen?"

"Yeah, Dad," Leonard asked with a little grin, "is it an omen?"

"No, we're seeing a runaway tire and— oh gee, it's going over to the oncoming lane!"

"A car's coming, Dad!" shouted Leonard.

3

He's swerving, swerving. He missed it! He missed it!"

"It's slowing down," said Posie. " Look it's angling back toward the grass. It's going back down into the median!"

"It's stopping!" screamed Nina. Everyone but Eddie and Leonard cheered as the wheel twirled around in tighter and tighter little circles and finally flopped down in the grassy median.

"I knew we shouldn't be moving," Eddie repeated to himself.

Wes and Leonard retrieved the tire and

refastened it to the trailer with three lug nuts borrowed from the other wheel. Greasy and flustered they jumped back in the station wagon and gunned it back onto the freeway. "Those kids at the shop," Wes declared, "they don't know how to tighten a lug nut. Somebody could have gotten hurt."

"Dad," Eddie interjected, "don't you think we should..."

"Don't even say it, Eddie. We're not going back. Our neighborhood's not cutting it and with Pop's help I've got a definite lead on a job in Bemidji. Pop said they're opening a new wood processing plant outside of town and he knows the personnel director. Says I'm as good as in."

"So how long do we have to live with Grandpa and what's-her-name?" Eddie asked and signed at the same time.

"What's-her-name's name is Phoebe," answered Posie.

"So what is she?" asked Nina. "She's not our grandmother is she?"

"No," Wes said, "your grandmother died quite a few years ago. So Phoebe would be your step-grandmother."

"Do you think she'll be a wicked step-grandmother like in Cinderella?"

"Have no idea," shrugged Wes. "Never met her. And to answer your question, Eddie, we'll live with them long enough to get a couple paychecks in the bank. Then we'll get a place of our own. Maybe a month or so."

Eddie mulled over his near and uncertain

future. He thought over his options and there appeared to be few. He couldn't exactly jump out of the car at this speed and run home. Those other people were moving in by now anyway. It made him furious to think of some other kid living in his room. The other option would be, of course, to stay in the car and move to Bemidji and hate every minute of it forever.

Eddie looked over at Leonard, who was impatiently fast forwarding his tape player. An idea struck. Eddie grabbed a scrap of paper from the floor, scribbled a note and slipped it to Leonard. It read: "Don't know about you, but I'm giving Bemidji about a week. Then I'm splitting—back to Minneapolis. You with me?"

Not knowing what to think, Leonard turned around to see if his little brother was kidding. Eddie's unblinking stare told Leonard he wasn't. After a minute or so Leonard looked over and gave Eddie a casual nod. It was a pretty crazy idea, Eddie thought. But at the same time, he was flattered that his older brother thought him worthy and grown up enough to run away with him.

Eddie adored his big brother the way only little brothers can.

Nina adored Eddie the way only little sisters can adore their big brothers. Eddie and

Nina had learned a lot of the same things together, especially speaking and signing. When he was four and would arrive home from school with his new words and signs, the two year old Nina would learn them right on the spot. Eddie loved showing her the signs and having someone to talk to as much as Nina loved learning them. Over time she had become almost as fast and fluent in signing as her brother.

The anger Eddie felt over the forced move left little room for noticing that spring was opening all around them. The early March sky was a blue paler than robins' eggs, and cirrus clouds, like wisps of angel hair, blew along at their icy heights. Far below on the earth the strengthening sunlight collected itself to melt the snow off the east facing banks of the freeway. The snow of the west banks stayed frozen for the time being and still showed the brown dirt and grime from the thousands of splashing winter vehicles. Ice was still on the Mississippi River and would be for a couple weeks more. Flocks of birds soon would find their way along and above the same rivers to some northern sloughs, woods or meadows.

It seemed the car barely rolled past the last of the endless northern suburbs before it approached the exits for St. Cloud.

Leaning forward between her parents, Nina asked, "Is this Bemidji? Are we there?"

Wes and Posie looked around at their daughter and smiled. "No," laughed Posie, "it's still two hours or so away."

"Closer to three hours," corrected Wes. Rolling her eyes, Nina flopped back into her seat and resumed staring out the window.

Eddie thought to himself. Three hours plus the hour we've already gone. Four hours! How would he and Leonard find their way back to Minneapolis from so far away?

After another hour or so, Eddie began to notice more and more pine trees and fewer of the bare branched, fat leafed trees. Weathered resort signs became common once they exited onto highway 71 at Sauk Centre. They were covered with pictures of loons or ducks or giant green fish with hooks and fishlines attached to their mouths. Eddie's spirits sank as he passed each new sign, because they showed he was getting closer and closer to the hated Bemidji and farther and farther from home.

Chapter Two

In silence they drove on through one tiny town after another, none with more than one gas station. The towns had names like Little Sauk, Browerville, Eagle Bend and Bertha. Eventually, they rolled into the outskirts of Bemidji.

Eddie could feel himself tense up. "Looks like every other building is a real estate office," remarked Wes. "You'd think . . ."

"Look at that!" shouted Nina who was now fully awake.

Startled, Wes slammed on the brake pedal and nearly sent the trailer into a skid.

"What?" Posie asked turning around to her daughter.

"Over there. Look at that!" Nina exclaimed. Off to their right, Eddie beheld two gigantic statues. One was a fifty foot, stiff looking statue of a man in a brilliantly colored red plaid shirt and blue jeans. He wore a funny hat that looked like a stovepipe with a baseball visor on the front. He smoked a little pipe and sported a mustache that extended probably six feet from end to end.

"Is that his pet or something?" Nina asked. "Why would he have a giant blue cow for a pet?"

For only the second time during the entire trip Leonard spoke up. "It's an ox."

"A what?" frowned Nina.

Leonard sighed, "It's supposed to be Paul Bunyon and Babe, the Blue Ox. I had to give a report on him last year. We were studying folklore."

"I heard of Paul Bunyon," said Eddie. "Wasn't he the giant that helped the loggers cut down trees?"

"Yeah," continued Leonard, "the lumberjacks made up stories about him for years. He could do all these great giant things. The legend says that all the ten thousand lakes in Minnesota were made from Paul's footprints that filled up with water. And the reason there aren't any trees in North Dakota is because Paul chopped them all down so he could have a place to lie down. There was even one story that said to unjam a pile of logs in the river, Paul walked Babe, the Blue Ox into the river. Then from shore he shot his rifle at Babe. Now Babe thought the bullets were flies and started spinning her tail. But it was so powerful it acted like a propeller and pushed the water and the logs back up the river."

Eddie, though trying to watch his brother's speech, was also watching the town of Bemidji pass by his window. What a stupid town, he

10

thought.

After passing through Bemidji and about half way to the next town of Black Duck, the LaVoi family rolled left off 71 onto a gravel road called County 15. The thawing road was uneven at best. There were ruts and muck holes and standing water in the low spots.

They rattled past one of Minnesota's dozens of lakes named Turtle Lake with newly formed puddles on it's surface from the melting ice. The Chevy splashed through the town of Puposky and veered east. Moving at a good clip on another gravel road, Eddie's father dodged puddles and ruts for two miles and quickly jerked the Chevy to the right onto a one-lane road that was mostly sand.

"Wes!" Posie shrieked hanging onto her door handle, "Why are you driving so fast? We're going to end up in a ditch out here in the middle of nowhere!"

Wes chuckled. "Trust me. I was raised here. You learn early in the spring when the roads are soft, you don't slow down for anything. Not unless you want to be buried up to your axles in mud."

"Dad," Nina said with a look of worry about her, "are you sure you're going the right way? There're no houses or, or anything out this

11

way. Who will we play with?"

"Each other, for the time being," said Posie. "At least until school starts again. The spring break for the schools up here, put at the end of your spring break, gives you about three weeks off. It's going to give you some time to get settled."

Eddie, meanwhile, attentively watched every turn and landmark. Everything passed so quickly and looked so much the same he wasn't sure he'd ever be able to find his way out. Eddie glanced over to see Leonard sleeping soundly, his mouth was wide open. He wouldn't be much help finding and retracing the roads back to Bemidji, thought Eddie.

At last, Wes pulled the wagon off the narrow sandy road onto an even narrower and sandier road. Branches of trees swished and clicked against the sides of the Chevy. Following the road back for a quarter mile or so they came into a clearing in the woods. Eddie saw the opening was about 150 feet across at the widest part. Placed in the center of the opening was a small, one story house with a TV antenna as high as the lot was wide. To the left of the house and pressed back against some bare trees was a low crooked shed made of gray corrugated metal. To the right rear of the house was a garage closed on three sides and open in the front. On one side of the garage was parked a powder blue pickup that looked to date back to the fifties. Three quarters of an inch of caked-on, yellow, spring mud coated the bottom half of the truck. Three or four cords of clean white birch logs, all split, dried and ready for burning lay stacked near the truck.

A dozen chickens and an arrogant looking rooster pecked the ground in the open places where the sun had been able to collect and burn off the snow. The rooster, alerted by the commotion, eyed the suspicious car.

"We're all going to stay in there?" asked Nina.

"It is a little smaller than I imagined," added Posie.

Eyeing his father in the rear view mirror, Eddie saw genuine surprise on his face. "I remember it being a lot bigger when I was living here," said Wes shaking his head.

Posie looked at her husband. "You a little nervous?"

"Na! . . .Well, yeah, some," Wes said getting out of the car and stretching. He leaned his head back into the car. "I talked to him on the phone for the first time after all these years. It's going to be okay."

Posie turned to address her children.

13

"Now remember, we're guests here for a while. Use your best manners. Help out with whatever chores there are. Not too much noise. Clean up after yourselves. It's going to be a little cramped for the time being, but we'll have our own place in no time." With that Posie and Nina joined Wes outside the car.

"Leonard, wake up," Eddie coaxed, tapping his brother on the knee. "We're here."

The older boy frowned, blinked his eyes several times and slowly sat up. Looking around the yard Leonard muttered some words that Eddie could see were bad ones. Eddie watched Leonard's face as his brother flopped back on the seat and pretended to go back to sleep. "I'm going back to sleep and dream of Minneapolis, Eddie. Wake me up later, but only if I'm in a place that's inhabited."

Leave a place for me in that dream, Eddie thought to himself.

Chapter Three

A stocky man with a military type hair cut stepped onto the front porch. He wore a baggy cardigan sweater and smoked a pipe.

Eddie watched his father outside the car. "I can't believe how much older he looks," said Wes. "Looks pretty healthy, though."

"You probably look a lot older to him too," smiled Posie. "You've got a few of those white streaks yourself. That's you in thirty years, Wes."

"Looks like I could do a lot worse," Wes said as he moved toward the house.

"Hi ya, Pop," said Wes climbing the porch steps. "It's been a long time." He awkwardly shook his father's hand.

The older man nodded. "It's good you came in the spring. When you left all those years ago, it was toward the end of winter. We'll just pick up where we left off like there were no seasons in between. Just winter to spring."

A quiet moment passed. "Pop, I told you about my wife, Posie. Posie this is my father, Ray LaVoi."

"You must be part Dakota," said Ray. "You're too tall to be Ojibwe."

"I'm half Dakota with a little Cherokee and

15

some Crow thrown in to make me a little sassy," said Posie "And this is our daughter, Nina. She's the baby."

While Nina blushed, Wes waved Eddie and Leonard up to the porch. Following his brother's lead, Eddie sulked out the door and sluggishly made his way toward the house. About half way to the house the red rooster that Eddie had seen as they drove up came rushing toward him at a full sprint. Though Eddie had never spent time around roosters, Eddie knew danger when he saw it. He spun around and bolted for the car as fast as his stiff traveler's legs would carry him. The bird's legs, unhappily for Eddie, were not stiff. Before Eddie could reach the door handle, the rooster was on him scratching and pecking as if Eddie were some mortal enemy. Suddenly, Eddie's grandfather was there shooing and slapping his arms at the rooster. Immediately, the bird stopped and ran back toward the other chickens.

"That bird," declared Eddie's grandfather shaking his head. "It's Phoebe's, and for some reason it's got a mean streak. It'll pick out one person and go after him like a coon after corn cobs. I'd shoot the durn bird if Phoebe wasn't so partial to it." Ray looked at Eddie who was pulling up his pant leg to examine his wounds.

16

"You okay, son?"

Eddie looked up and brushed his ink black hair from his eyes. "What did you say?"

"Are you okay, son?"

Eddie nodded and gritted his teeth as he saw two little teardrops of blood run down his leg.

Ray didn't see Eddie's wound. "Good. You can't let a bird get you on your heels." He clapped Eddie on the back and headed toward the others.

Eddie looked around for some comforting, but none was to be found since everyone was being introduced to Leonard. As Eddie limped up to the porch, keeping one eye on the rooster, he saw Phoebe come out of the house. She was a tiny woman with fierce black eyes that looked magnified by a pair of terrifically thick glasses. Her close cropped hair was tinted some reddish shade of the color orange.

"And this is Eddie," announced Wes. "He's our middle child."

"What's wrong with your leg?" Phoebe asked.

"It got scratched up and bit by that stupid rooster over there."

Ray, sensing things could take a bad turn, invited everyone inside. As the door opened, loud music poured out onto the porch. "Oh good,"

17

Leonard said rolling his eyes toward Eddie, " I just love country music."

Phoebe stopped in the doorway. "You do?" she said looking at Leonard hopefully. "Wes and I just can't get enough of it. We play it around here all day long. You and I are going to get along just fine. Here let me turn up this Wynonna tune. I just love this one. Can't that gal sing?"

Once seated in the tiny living room, Phoebe said to Eddie, "You know that rooster that come after you ain't stupid. He's smart, and not only that, he's a prize winner. His name is Robson and he won first prize at the Koochiching County Fair last year. You should have seen how much money people were offering me for that 'stupid' bird-as you call him."

"Well, I didn't mean so much he was stupid as much as I meant he was mean."

Phoebe didn't answer Eddie. Addressing her husband she said, "The boy talks kind of different. He ain't slow is he?"

Eddie's mother bristled. "No, he is not slow," she said sharply. "In fact, he's very bright. Eddie has a hearing problem. He's nearly deaf, but with his hearing aids and watching people's lips he does just fine."

Eddie felt his face flush with anger from Phoebe's remarks and from humiliation after

18

being attacked by a chicken. He vowed to himself that when Leonard was ready, he was going back home to Minneapolis. His own neighborhood couldn't be much more dangerous or unpleasant than this place.

Chapter Four

"I guess you two boys can sleep here in the den," said Phoebe. "One of you can pull the cushions off that couch and set up on the floor and the other can sleep on what's left of the couch."

Eddie and Leonard peeked into the tiny room that was just big enough for the couch, a little desk across from it and one step in between. By moving the palms of his hands with fingers pointing outward, closer together and then apart again, Eddie signed to Leonard that the room was too small. Leonard, although not as good at signing as Nina, knew quite a few of Eddie's signs. He nodded his agreement.

"What's that mean?" Phoebe demanded. "Is that some of that sign language stuff?"

"Yep," answered Leonard flashing a mock smile. "It means this room will do just fine."

Most of the afternoon was spent getting unpacked and acquainted. It was decided that Nina would share the second bedroom with her parents on a small army cot.

That night Leonard got to stay up later with the grown-ups and Nina decided to drag her sleeping bag into the den with Eddie instead of being all by herself in her parent's bedroom. Scooting over to the doorway, she listened in on the adults' conversation and signed everything to Eddie.

Most of the talk was about local folks their father had known growing up and what they had been up to lately—mostly boring stuff Eddie decided. This went on for about twenty minutes. Eddie was about to tell his sister she could stop interpreting when she signed that their father was asking Ray a question. "So Pop, who do I contact at the paper plant about the bookkeeper job? I'd like to get over there tomorrow. The sooner I get started the better."

There was a pause in Nina's signing before she began signing her grandfather's response. "I didn't know how to bring this up, Wes. Just today--in fact you were on your way up here and. . ." Again Nina paused. "I called up this fellow I know at the plant to set up a time for you to come in." Ray paused. "Son, I don't know how to tell you this, but he said he was real sorry, but he gave the job to someone else."

Quickly, Eddie slid alongside his sister and watched his father down the hallway. Their father stared straight ahead without saying a word. Then abruptly, he stood up, walked to the door and turned back toward the room. "Pop, I dragged my whole family, kicking and howling, pulled the kids out of school, away from their friends and. . and you're telling me that the job—the sure thing-wasn't so sure after all?"

"I'm just going by what I was told," said Ray raising his voice. "I was told it was a sure thing. How am I supposed to know he's going to up and give the job to some kid with a college degree from Bemidji State."

"Yeah, well did you tell him I had a degree from vocational school and six years of experience?"

"Sure," Ray answered excitedly. "I told him all that. He'd seen your resume and all. He was a little nervous because the company you worked for went belly up."

"Yeah, Pop, but that had nothing to do with my bookkeeping. It was because this auto tune-up company I worked for tried to cut costs by hiring kids who didn't know a spark plug from an alternator. I can't believe this. This friend of yours thinks somehow I'm responsible?"

Silence floated between the two men for a long moment. "I'll keep my ear to the ground," the older man said. "I know lots of people."

"I hope they're more reliable than this other friend of yours," Wes said sharply. Then he turned to Leonard who had been watching wide-eyed. He had rarely seen his father this worked up. "And we're not going back to Minneapolis! Tomorrow, I'm dropping off the U-Haul, buying a paper, and looking for a job. So, we can all finish unpacking."

"I'll be coming too," Posie added. "I've worked all my life, too. We'll find something. I think we should go for a walk now and cool off."

"Yeah, yeah I think that's a good idea," agreed Wes. Posie brought the coats, and Eddie watched his parents step out the front door into the brisk black night. As bad as Eddie felt for his father, he couldn't help feel a little glimmer of hope that things might not work out in Bemidji and they would have to move back to Minneapolis.

"So," Leonard said to Wes and Phoebe, trying to change the subject. He looked desperately around the room for topics. On the walls were a few inexpensive prints of large fish jumping out of the water, a white tail deer about to bolt, and a moose with a bushel of swamp slop hanging from it's rack. There were small framed photos on the coffee table of someone whom Leonard took to be his grandfather dressed in a military uniform. "Grandfather, is that you?" questioned Leonard.

"Sure is," Ray answered brightening some.

"It was taken when I was in the Marines. It was during World War II. You ever seen that picture of the soldiers raising the flag on Iwo Jima?"

Leonard looked up respectfully. "You were one of those soldiers?"

"No, but I was there," laughed Ray. "I saw them taking the picture from below the hill. Funny thing. They had to do it a couple times. They wanted it to be unnerving for the enemy, so they wanted to be sure to set it up in a good position. It was a pretty impressive sight. Of course, we never thought it would become such a famous scene."

Eddie saw Nina was tiring of trying to sign so quickly. "Keep going. Keep going," Eddie signed to his sister." She sighed and turned back down the hallway.

"Now Ray," Phoebe interrupted, "don't get carried away with those war stories. We'll be here all night. Did I tell you about how I came to get my rooster, Robson?"

Phoebe dove into a torturously long and detailed story about how she had spotted Robson. Phoebe could see his prize winning potential when Robson was still a chick, and she got that bird for an unbelievable price. And, of course, it was worth a small fortune now. When Phoebe finally ended her tale and headed to the bathroom, Nina

24

toppled over onto the floor to show how exhausted she was from signing. Later as Eddie drifted toward slumber, his mind replayed little scenes from the day: the Minneapolis skyline, the note to Leonard, Paul Bunyan, Robson's attack, his father's job falling through. Then he reviewed the chores each of them would have. Nina would help with inside chores and any snow shoveling that might come up. Leonard would be in charge of hauling wood for the stove.

Eddie was expected to feed the chickens once a day and bring in eggs every morning. He would also be expected to help with dishes and help Leonard split wood if he got behind. Sleep didn't come easily. Images of Robson charging and tormenting him kept Eddie from a restful and peaceful sleep.

Chapter Five

No one in Eddie's family slept well that night. Eddie's parents had walked together for over an hour and came quietly into the still, but uneasy household. From the footsteps vibrating the wooden floors, Eddie was roused from his sleep. In the dark Eddie could see Leonard listening to his radio. Aside from worrying about the rooster, Eddie wondered to himself about money. Did his parents have enough for the family. They'd never had a lot of money, but both his parents had worked pretty steadily ever since he could remember. He knew they couldn't have a lot of cash saved up if they were living with his grandfather.

He fretted about school too. Good old Seward School. Minneapolis was a big city— big enough for a program with other hard of hearing kids, where they could take regular classes with hearing kids. It was possible because there were interpreters who could sign what the teachers were saying. Eddie was sure there wouldn't be anything that could measure up to what he was used to. Mrs. McMahan had been his teacher for the hard of hearing. She knew

Eddie and his needs and moods and talents and shortcomings. Well, there just couldn't be anyone like that up in Bemidji. He pictured himself sticking out like a sore thumb— a thumb wearing a hearing aid. He'd be the odd new kid.

The next morning was overcast, but warm for early March. It was still dark when Eddie was awakened by thumping footsteps on the floor and by an aching back. By a flip of the coin, Eddie had lost and been forced to sleep on the sofa cushions on the floor. Leonard claimed he had called tails, but claimed Eddie didn't hear him. During the night, the cushions had slid apart and while his shoulders and legs were up on the cushions, his hips were on the bare floor. Eddie got up on his knees, rubbed his back and looked on the couch for his brother. No Leonard. Kneeling on the couch, Eddie leaned his nose against the icy window pane and cupped the sides of his face. In the blush-pink morning light Eddie could make out the form of his brother lightly stepping over the crunchy snow that had refrozen during the night.

Eddie suddenly remembered he had chicken duty. Oh no, he thought. That stupid rooster. Dressing quickly, Eddie hoped he could have the protection of his big brother while Leonard was still outside gathering wood.

By the time Eddie found his clothes and coat and stepped out of the back door, Leonard was coming up the back steps with an armload of logs. Leonard motioned with his head for Eddie to hold the door. Stepping quickly past Eddie, Leonard dumped the white, split logs into a round metal tub. The logs clunking heavily onto the bottom of the tub sounded like pounding on a kettle drum even to Eddie. Leonard looked around with a satisfied expression and brushed off his hands.

"Hey, Leonard," said Eddie with a smile. "I've got to do the chickens. Do you want to come with me—and maybe help?"

"Naw, not today. I'm starved and I'm done with my chores. You just got to dump some feed and water and bring in the eggs, right?"

Eddie nodded.

"So hustle back with those eggs. I could eat a dozen myself. I went for a walk before I got the wood. You know, it's kind of nice out there. I mean, all the trees and everything. And it's quiet--almost spooky quiet. Anyway, get the eggs. The air up here makes me hungry."

Looking around to assure himself that no adults were coming, Eddie signed, "We're still cutting out of here, right? In a few days, you said, right?"

Leonard paused as if he were remembering something. "Oh yeah, definitely." He slid a piece of bread into the toaster and snapped the lever down. "Yep, definitely. A few days."

Feeling hope, Eddie converted it to courage. He headed out the back door to tackle the chickens. Just outside the back door, Eddie found a tin bucket. After chipping a layer of ice from the bottom of the bucket, Eddie refilled it with frigid water from the outside faucet. Cautiously, he moved across the yard toward the chicken coop, thinking that he never knew a bucket of water could be so heavy. He remembered Robson and felt the scabs on his ankle pull with each step. The chicken coop was closed up at night so there would be protection from the fox and mink that would kill every chicken in a matter of minutes.

Eddie set the bucket down near the door and rubbed his fingers where the handle had dug into his hand. Eddie ever so slowly pulled the door open, all the while keeping himself hidden behind it. It creaked noisily on its rusty hinges. Peeking through the crack where the door hinged, Eddie waited for the better part of a minute. Finally, he saw the rusty colored Robson slowly strut down the little gangway to the ground. One by one, the hens with their dirty white feathers cautiously followed the rooster out into the yard. Eddie breathed easier, but kept his eyes on Robson. When the bird moved behind a tree, Eddie stepped out from behind the door. Suddenly, the door made a loud squeak on its worn hinges. Robson darted out from behind the tree and eyed a startled Eddie.

Their eyes locked. Robson immediately charged. Eddie's eyes grew wide and for just a moment he froze. Then simple fear kicked Eddie into gear. The door! he thought. Eddie ducked into the low doorway of the chicken coop and slammed the door behind him. The sounds of Robson fussing came from outside the door.

Eddie's fear was soon replaced. Growing up in the city, he had never been exposed to the pleasantries of the inside of a chicken coop. The dry, choking stench of the air made him gag and he was grateful he hadn't eaten breakfast.

Deciding to take care of his business as swiftly as possible, Eddie found the feed. It was stored in a big steel drum. He refilled the feed trays all the while trying to breathe as little as possible. Next, he thought, the water. It was still outside the coop. The best way to get the water, he thought, was to go as fast as possible before Robson could get back to the door. Eddie jerked the door open, which alerted Robson. On came the bird. Eddie reached out with one arm and yanked the bucket into the coop. Water splashed up on Robson's wiggly red rooster face just as he arrived at the door. The frigid water stunned the rooster just long enough to allow Eddie to reclose the door. He quickly refilled the drinking trays and searched the nests for eggs. He picked up the half dozen eggs he found and put then in a little pouch he made by pulling up the bottom of his sweatshirt. Turning toward the door, Eddie felt himself getting light-headed from the odor and from trying hard not to breathe.

Squatting down by the door, Eddie cracked the door enough to see Robson over in the side yard pecking at the ground and looking oblivious. Now, besides feeling light-headed, Eddie was getting sick to his stomach. He knew he couldn't stay in the coop much longer. He'd have to make a run for it.

With the eggs pressed against his stomach with one hand and the bucket held in the other, Eddie burst from the chicken coop like a desperate bank robber making a get-away. The door banged off the wall. He gasped at the fresh air and ran as fast and as clumsily as he'd ever run in his life.

All the commotion was not lost on Robson, who, after being startled for an instant, shot after Eddie. Seeing the rooster streaking after him,

Eddie kicked his speed a notch higher. The eggs wiggled and shook against his belly while the empty bucket bounced against his knee. Eddie eyed the back step and tried not to think of the gaining rooster.

Just when he thought he might have a chance to make it, Eddie's foot found a patch of refrozen ice. Eddie's foot slipped forward and he almost flipped onto his back. He righted himself and got his weight forward. But Eddie had adjusted too far and at the same time he caught his foot on a ridge of crusty snow. The bucket flew out of his hand and Eddie flopped forward onto his stomach. Eddie heard the crunching of eggs beneath him and then the sound of crashing glass.

Eddie lay there and covered his head. He waited with eyes closed for the attack. Nothing happened. Slowly Eddie moved one arm, then the other. He checked his legs. Right. Left. Okay. Slowly, Eddie sat up and looked up toward the back door. The noisy crash of the bucket through glass had scared Robson off. But the noise had alerted someone else. Eddie saw pink curlers in orange hair. Glaring at him from behind a broken storm window and holding the tin bucket was a very unhappy Phoebe.

Chapter Six

With their parents out job hunting, the rest of the day went slowly for the LaVoi children. Early in the afternoon Leonard told Eddie, "Come on. Let's take a walk up the road. If I play one more game of cards I'll scream."

"I don't want to," replied Eddie. "I want to do some drawing."

"You're just scared of the rooster," accused Nina. Noticing Eddie's sudden glare she added, "That's okay, though. I'm scared of things, too. Not roosters, but other things. Leonard, I'm getting our coats."

"I'm not scared," Eddie protested to his sister as she left the room. "And besides, you never got pecked and scratched up by him. I'm the only one he seems to hate. Well, I hate him too. I'm not scared of him. I hate him."

"You can draw later," Leonard said. "I think Nina's right about the rooster. I've heard of people being chicken before, but I never heard of someone being chicken of chickens." Leonard zipped up his jacket as Nina headed out the back door.

"I'm drawing a picture of a big, four course chicken dinner," Eddie said ignoring his brother's

comment. "I'll go for a walk some other time."
Eddie looked around to be sure no one was near.
"Besides, a couple more days and we'll be out of
here. When we're back home, we'll take a walk
down to the Colonel's Kentucky Fried and I'll
buy you a chicken dinner."
"Fine. See you later. "

When Wes and Posie returned that evening,
Eddie discovered his mother had found a
minimum wage job. "I'll be working at a place
called Big B Bait and Laundromat. I'll be selling
minnows and worms and such. I haven't fished
since I was a kid."
Wes hadn't had much luck—a few
"maybes" and a couple "we'll-get-back-to-yous."
He was quiet the rest of the night.
On the positive side, Eddie learned that
Phoebe locked the chickens up each night. So
for most of the evening Eddie devised a plan for
safely handling his chore the next morning. He
reminded himself that another couple days and
there would be no more chicken chores or chicken
sores.
The next morning Eddie went outside at
first light. Once at the chicken coop he leaned a
log against its front wall and climbed onto the
roof. Lying with his head out over the front edge,

he reached down with the hooked end of an unraveled coat hanger. Then Eddie hooked the latch and pulled up. The door popped loose and he reached down to swing the door open. When the chickens finally had wandered out and Robson was well away from the coop, Eddie jumped off the roof. He grabbed the bucket of water and slipped inside. Then he reached into his pocket and pulled out a cotton dish towel to wrap around his nose and mouth.

Once the water, feed, and eggs were taken care of, Eddie was set for the get-away. When Eddie spotted Robson looking the other way, he slipped out the door with his bucket and clambered back onto the roof. There he waited for a few minutes until Robson meandered behind a tree. Jumping off the back edge of the roof, Eddie tiptoed into the woods. From there he made his way back toward the house, scampering from tree to tree along side the yard. Had Eddie not been watching so attentively for Robson, he wouldn't have banged the bucket on a tree trunk. Instantly, the rooster spun his head around in the direction of the sound. The prey and predator locked eyes.

Bursting out of the brush, Eddie tore for the house with just a little less speed than he needed. Eddie arrived at the back door with a new set of scratches to his legs and to his pride. I'm for sure getting out of this crazy place, Eddie promised himself. And soon.

As he lay in bed the next morning before his egg duty, Eddie hatched another idea. Roosters can't fly, he thought to himself. If he could protect his legs from Robson, he'd be all right. On his way to the chicken coop, Eddie dragged along an empty steel garbage can he'd seen in the shed. He set it next to the door of the coop, climbed up on the roof and waited. When the chickens were out, Eddie slipped inside and discovered five eggs. He wrapped each one in kleenex and slipped them into the pockets of his jacket.

After filling the feed and water, Eddie slipped out the door and climbed into the garbage can. He grabbed the handles of the can and began hopping toward the house like a rabbit. The metal can banged on the frozen ground and made such a racket that all the chickens, but Robson, scattered to the other side of the house. Eddie was beginning to feel smug about his plan. He hopped along with his metal bucket clanging on the sides of the garbage can. Robson stared as if Eddie were some kind of strange metallic bobbing robin.

"Na, na, na, boo, boo, you stupid bird,"

Eddie sang to the rooster. "Can't get me."

Although his wings were clipped, Robson suddenly ran full speed toward Eddie and somehow became airborne. Eddie didn't even have time to scream. He instantly ducked down inside the garbage can, just as the flailing fowl blew over him. The sudden movement caused Eddie to topple over. Out of the can he tumbled. He scrambled to his feet, and lit off for the house with wet eggs oozing from his pockets and Robson in hot pursuit pecking at his flying heels.

When Eddie reached the house he saw an old man step around the corner. "Help," cried Eddie. The stranger, moving quickly for an old man, stepped around Eddie, waved off Robson and shooed him away. Biting his lower lip, Eddie sat down on the step to study the new set of scratches to go along with the older scabbed ones and the ones still under band-aids.

Sighing, Eddie looked up at the man who'd

rescued him. The man had long, silver, straight hair worn in the old Indian way—pulled back and tied in a pony tail. His chestnut colored face was deeply lined, especially around the eyes. The eyes looked unusual to Eddie. Instead of being dark brown, like most Indians, his eyes were a pale gray, like the color of weathered fencing. The man looked to Eddie like one of the oldest people he'd ever seen, yet he was solidly built with large strong hands. He was dressed in baggy, khaki pants and a flannel shirt.

"Thanks Mister," said Eddie. "Those roosters are faster than they look." The old man looked blankly at Eddie for a moment. Eddie repeated his thank you. The old man, watching Eddie's face, warmly nodded his understanding. Then stepping around Eddie, he headed up the steps and walked right in the back door.

Following the man into the house, Eddie heard Phoebe say, "Tom, don't you ever knock?" Then she called out to Eddie's grandfather. "Ray, your father's here—again."

Father? Eddie thought to himself. Grandfather Ray's father? That would make that old man . . . my, great-grandfather. I didn't even know I had one.

Running into his parents room, Eddie woke them. "Hey, Dad."

"What?" Wes opened one eye and rolled over.

"Knock, knock."

"Oh, please," complained Wes pulling the pillow over his head.

"Come on," Eddie pleaded and pulled the pillow off his father's head. "Knock, knock."

"Okay, but then you let me sleep. Uh, who's there?"

"Old man."

"Um, old man, who?"

"Old man out in the kitchen with long hair and I think he's my great-grandfather."

Wes sat up in bed. "Gray Eyes?" Wes asked.

"No," replied Eddie. "Phoebe called him Tom."

"Gray Eyes is his Indian name. It's his given Ojibwe name. Tom is the name the missionaries gave him. Wow! I've been out of touch with the family for so long, I thought . . . I assumed he was dead."

"He looks alive to me," Eddie declared. "He looks very old, but very alive."

"Yeah, about ninety-something years alive," added Wes.

Chapter Seven

Four generations of LaVoi men stood facing each other in the kitchen. Eddie, Leonard, and Nina watched their father and grandfather as they tried to carry on a conversation with Gray Eyes. It was clear to Eddie that Gray Eyes wasn't hearing most of what was being said. From his own experience he knew that for a person with hearing problems it was hard to follow a conversation with more than one or two people. The conversational ball kept being thrown from person to person. It was difficult for Gray Eyes to know who was speaking, and so it made it hard to read the mouth of the speaker. There were other interfering noises in the room like running water and Phoebe's chattering. Eddie felt sympathy for the man. He'd been through it himself hundreds of times. Eddie signed over to Nina, "He's like me. He can't hear too well." Eddie could see the look of frustration growing on Gray Eye's face.

Nina signed to Eddie, "He's not wearing a hearing aid. How do you know?"

"I know," Eddie said touching his forehead with the tips of his right hand. Eddie watched his great-grandfather. To Eddie it looked like Gray Eyes was tiring of working so hard to carry on a conversation without enough sound. Bit by bit, Gray Eyes backed out of the conversation by letting Ray and Wes carry it. Eddie saw that Gray Eyes had noticed Nina and him briskly chatting to each other with their hands.

When Eddie looked up and saw his great-grandfather watching, he gave the man a shy wave.

Gray Eyes, without smiling, gave Eddie a slight nod, turned, and headed for the door. "I've got to be going," he said without looking up. He picked his coat off the hook and headed out the door.

Eddie's family watched the door for a few moments. "Pop, why did he leave so soon?" Eddie's father asked. "I haven't seen the man in over twenty years. Shoot, I didn't even know he was alive." Wes walked over to watch his grandfather walk along the back of the house, climb into an old pickup and drive away.

"Dad's going kinda deaf," explained Ray. "Can't hardly hear a thing unless you practically shout right at him. He doesn't do too bad if he can see you're talking to him. Kind of worries me though. He's not seeing people like he used to."

Phoebe chimed in. "Not seeing people, either? I didn't know that. It's bad enough he can't hear, but now he can't see them either?"

"No, no," Ray protested. "His sight's okay. What I mean is he's not visiting and hanging out with his old buddies so much any more. Since his hearing's gone down hill, he's kind of withdrawn. He used to come over and play that old moccasin game. Remember that game where he hid the stones under the moccasin, Wes?"

Eddie's father smiled. "I'd forgotten about that. We used to play that every time he'd come over."

Ray continued. "Dad used to come over here at least a couple times a week to visit. Now, maybe he stops in once every week or two, and then he stays just a few minutes and off he goes. Some of his old friends say they haven't seen much of him lately. He just sets out there at the reservation in his little house doing—I don't know what."

"I'd like to see him again," said Eddie's father.

"Maybe I'll ask him to come back Sunday for breakfast," said Ray. "I'll swing by on my way to town and ask him tomorrow."

Phoebe cut in. "You know, he seems to hear just fine when he wants to." She wiped her hands on a kitchen towel. "Appears to me he hears okay sometimes and other times he don't. I'm not so sure I agree with that doctor he seen. I just wonder if he don't hear when he feels like it. The doctor told him he needs a hearing aid, but he won't have nothing to do with it. The man's over ninety for crying out loud. He doesn't have to worry about looking too old."

"Now, Phoebe, I don't agree," argued Wes. "He doesn't care about looking old. He's always been sold on the old ways of doing things and, well, a hearing aid . . . he just doesn't feel it's natural. He won't have a TV you know."

Nina cleared her throat. "I think I know why he can hear some people better. Some voices are lower and softer—and others—" Nina tried not to look at Phoebe— "other voices kind of cut through everything and stick out." Nina thought for a moment. "Sort of how a smoke alarm is easy to hear."

"Yeah, I can hear Phoebe's voice the best," chimed in Eddie.

No one in the room said a thing until they saw how Phoebe would take what Eddie said. The old woman watched Eddie's face for a few moments to see if Eddie was trying to insult her. Eddie's face maintained its innocent expression. Eddie looked around and saw everyone watching him.

"I said something stupid didn't I? I didn't

mean to."

Phoebe folded her dish towel, slapped it on the kitchen counter, and strode out of the room.

By the end of the week, Phoebe finally began to warm to Eddie's extra kindnesses. Wes' job hunting had not warmed up at all. Each evening he'd come home a bit quieter than the day before. Posie's job went all right for such a low paying job. Nina told Eddie that each night before turning in she heard their parents discussing in low tones how they would pay for food and other bills unless Wes found something pretty soon.

During the day while their parents were gone, Leonard and Nina went for long walks up and down the gravel road. Each day upon their return, Leonard would tell Eddie about a new sighting of a bird, animal or set of strange tracks. Excitedly, he would draw them on a piece of paper and have Ray identify the animal. By the end of the week they had seen tracks of deer, a raccoon, a skunk and a red fox. Leonard and Nina had actually seen a barred owl swoop silently across the road and a hawk staring down from a power line.

The enthusiastic look on Leonard's face after his walks began to worry Eddie. It didn't look like the face of someone who was about to move back to Minneapolis. Aside from his fears of Robson, Eddie avoided the walks because he didn't want to give himself any chance to start liking the area. Instead, he spent his days drawing, watching TV, and looking at every picture over a twenty year span of National Geographic Magazine.

On Friday night when he and Leonard were getting ready for bed, Eddie brought up the subject of leaving. Speaking softly he asked, "Leonard, we're still going back, aren't we? You know, home. Minneapolis."

Leonard looked surprised as if he hadn't thought about it lately. "Sure. Yeah. Pretty soon. I'll let you know."

"When?" pleaded Eddie. "You said just a few days. I hate it here."

Squirming into his sleeping bag, Leonard replied, "You have to get off your tail once in a while and get out, little brother. It's kind of nice around here." Leonard paused. "Did I tell you we found a lake about two miles down the road?"

Eddie ignored his brother. Angrily, he pulled his sleeping bag over his head and rolled so his back was toward Leonard.

The only thing good that had happened all week was that Phoebe had fired Eddie from his chicken duties. She complained that too many eggs were being broken, the feed was spilled everywhere and the water bucket was usually someplace out in the middle of the yard. Eddie knew it was all true. He was reassigned to cleaning any floor covered with linoleum. This was just fine with him.

Eddie still refused to go outside, yet the rooster lay in waiting most of the time. Part of the time Robson scouted the backyard as if trying to keep the back door in sight. The other part of the time Eddie didn't know where the rooster went. Eddie would check out all the windows and couldn't see the bird anywhere.

Saturday morning Eddie made the mistake of agreeing to run down the driveway to get the mail. Robson was nowhere to be seen. About halfway to the mailbox the bird exploded out from under the front porch and chased Eddie into his grandfather's parked pickup truck. There he waited for the better part of an hour studying the truck's dashboard and examining all the contents of the glove compartment. Finally, the rooster left for the other side of the yard and Eddie scampered back into the house.

That evening, after the kitchen was cleaned up to Phoebe's satisfaction, Ray ordered everyone

46

into the station wagon.

"Good!" proclaimed Nina tightening her seat belt between her parents. "I've got cabin fever. I don't care where we go. We can go to the dump or to watch trees grow. Anywhere. It doesn't matter. I'm ready."

"Where are we going?" Eddie inquired.

"It's sort of a secret," said Ray, "but I'll give you a hint. It'd help if you had your dancing shoes on."

Chapter Eight

A light snow fell as the family bounced northward on the gravel road. They moved onto a blacktop road for some fifteen minutes or so until Eddie saw a sign that said, 'Now Entering Red Lake Reservation.' A short time later they approached a small town, turned a corner and pulled up at what looked to Eddie like a small high school. A few people were leisurely entering the building.

"They never quite start at seven so I think we'll find a place to sit," said Ray. Once they had made their way to the gym, Eddie saw an explosion of color before him. Scattered around the basketball court were people dressed in varied and colorful dancing costumes. The reds, blues, oranges and turquoises swam over the wooden floor. Spectacular feathers and painstakingly wonderful beaded jewelry dangled and twisted from the dancers as they prepared for their performances.

In the center of the floor a group of five men set up a huge drum. It was decorated with a blue band on its side near the bottom. "The four heads outlined in red," explained Ray, "represent the four Mide Manido—one for each of the directions: north, east, west and south. The oblong

48

line outlined in blue stands for a bag containing yarrow, a flowering plant. It signifies life."

"What about the sticks?" asked Leonard. "They're all carved into something."

"If you look closely at the drumming sticks you can see they are carved in the shape of a loon's head. See the eyes? Sometimes they are in the shape of an owl, but the loon is better. It was the first bird selected to form part of the Mide beliefs."

"What's Mide?" Nina asked her grandfather.

"Mide has to do with the traditional religious beliefs of the Ojibwe people."

Down on the floor Eddie saw several men bring folding chairs to the drum. They were big men, who wore their hair long in the old way, like Gray Eyes. The men wore serious looks.

Eventually, the men took their seats and immediately began beating the drum in a driving one-two count. Their voices rose in a loud, high pitched song rendered in the Ojibwe language. One by one the dancers began their choreography.

Eddie wasn't in the mood for festivities and pageantry. He was beginning to think that Leonard was weakening on his plan to return to Minneapolis. He wasn't encouraged when he looked over and saw his brother tapping his foot and watching the dancers like he was really enjoying it.

Round and round the dancers moved, each with a different style. Each felt and interpreted the dance in his or her own way. Some bobbed and spinned in feverishly quick motions with bells jingling from the toes of their moccasins. Others moved like sly animals stalking some invisible prey, while some pranced proudly like brilliantly colored birds. Several dancers stepped serenely, taking two short steps with the right foot and two steps with the left foot. Many of the performers seemed driven to entertain; others were quietly into their own experience and interpretation of the music.

All of the pageantry was lost on Eddie, whose thoughts were far away. He was brought back when he saw Leonard get up and move off the bleachers. Leonard worked his way across the front of the seats, along the baseline of the court and off to the far corner where some girls, about Leonard's age, were preparing to join the dancers. Eddie watched his brother walk right up and start talking with them.

Through narrowed eyes Eddie watched his brother's lips. Leonard was learning their names and where they went to school. He could see the girls laughing at some of the clever things Leonard said. Soon the girls were showing him some traditional dance steps and encouraging him after his first awkward attempts. Eddie did not like what he saw. Leonard was enjoying himself.

During a break between dances, Wes and Posie found an old friend and were soon engaged in a lively conversation. Eddie saw his father's face looking brighter than he'd seen it since the job hunting had begun.

"Eddie, come on over here. I want you to meet an old friend of mine. This is Butch. Well, I call him Butch. His name is Michael Dunkirk."

"People still call me Butch. That's fine with me," said the tall slender man. "Nice to meet you Eddie." The man extended his hand. "You know when your father and I were your age, we were just like this." Butch held two slender fingers together.

Forcing a smile, Eddie said, "Yeah, me and Kyle are kind of like that." Then looking away he corrected himself, "Or we were like that. My friend Kyle lives back in Minneapolis where we used to live."

Butch said something else, but Eddie wasn't listening or watching. Instead he drifted off while his father resumed his conversation with Butch. With a long face Eddie sat on one of the bottom bleachers and watched some young men hauling in guitars and amplifiers for another kind

51

of dance.

A few minutes later he watched Leonard walk up and ask his parents something. With Leonard's back turned toward him he didn't pick up what was being said. He did see that Leonard was happy to get permission to do something.

Back at the house it was sometime after midnight when Eddie was awakened by the commotion of Leonard's footsteps. He had stayed for the young people's dance. In the faint light from the hallway light, Eddie could see his brother reviewing some of the new dance steps he'd learned. Although he was half asleep, Eddie was still angry with his brother and kicked out his feet as Leonard stepped by.

"Ouch!" Leonard protested in a muffled voice. He closed the door and flicked on the light switch.

"You almost stepped on me," said Eddie.

"Yeah, but I didn't," Leonard signed angrily. "I saw you there. So what's your problem?"

Eddie sat up and looked accusingly at his brother. "You're my problem!"

"Me? I'm not the one with the problem. You're the one who mopes around here all day.

You don't do anything. You hardly talk to anyone. You haven't been outside in days. And you say I'm the one with the problem?"

Eddie waved off Leonard and flopped back on his sleeping bag.

"No," declared Leonard. "I want to know why you say I've got the problem."

Pursing his lips, Eddie thought for a moment. "You lied to me. You said we're leaving in a few days. The note in the car. Remember?" Eddie glared at his brother. "You aren't leaving are you?"

The older boy looked away. He shook his head.

"You promised me. You said we'd try it for a while and . . ."

"That was before. I kind of like it here. I like the trees and the wildlife."

"And that girl too," Eddie said accusingly.

"Yeah," Leonard said looking back at Eddie. "She's kind of nice. No, she's real nice and I met some other kids tonight. One of them even thought I should try out for the baseball team this spring. Back in Minneapolis the school was so big the team was next to impossible to make. I think I could play here. I can hit." Leonard swung an imaginary bat.

Tears began forming at the corners of

Eddie's eyes. Quickly, he turned off the light so Leonard wouldn't see. "I'm really happy for you," Eddie said sarcastically and fluffed his pillow with a few well placed punches.

Chapter Nine

The next morning could have been a good one for sleeping in, but Gray Eyes walked in the back door at sunrise. One by one, the slippered family members—minus Leonard, shuffled across the blue linoleum to the kitchen table. Ray put on the coffee pot and sent Nina out for the Sunday paper.

Positioning himself across the table from Gray Eyes, Eddie studied the man. To Eddie he seemed uncomfortable answering questions. Probably can't read speech very well, Eddie thought to himself. Most of his answers are short, and he doesn't ask many questions.

The last person to enter the room was Phoebe, who immediately shuffled across the floor, yanked open the refrigerator, and turned to Eddie. "Eggs. We need some." She pointed to the chicken coop. "Here's a carton. Don't break any this time or you'll be the one to go without. I'm giving you one more chance." Phoebe plopped a carton in front of Eddie.

Eddie looked up and found his great-grandfather studying him.

Gray Eyes saw fear in Eddie's eyes, though he was trying to hide it. A certain widening of the eyes and set of the mouth told the old man. He had seen it before. There was the time many years ago on the shores of Red Lake when he fished with his family. A tornado dropped out of the sky across the water and churned its way in their direction. To protect the children, his parents found a depression in the ground, lay their children in it and then laid on top of them. To keep from blowing off the children, they gripped the trunks of small saplings that grew along the shore. While the tornado with all its ferocity and flying debris spun around them, he saw fear.

The rooster was no tornado, but Gray Eyes knew that the size of the fear is not caused by the size of the enemy; it's caused by the victim feeling powerless.

Eddie silently slipped off his chair, took the egg carton, and slowly went out the back door. He stood on the back step desperately trying to come up with another plan. Quickly, Eddie came up with a new twist on the garbage can plan.

Eddie didn't see his great-grandfather watching from the window as he slipped under the upside down garbage can with the eggs. Lifting the can an inch or two off the turf, Eddie slid in the general direction of the house with the furious Robson circling. The rooster tried to peck at his feet beneath the rim. Things went well for a while. Except for the ground below him, Eddie couldn't see anything, including the very solid elm tree before him.

The crash caused Eddie to bounce and stagger backward. He managed to keep his feet for a few steps, but his heel caught on some crusty snow. Eddie tumbled onto his back with a metallic boom. He knew it was sure to be heard in the house.

The noise sent Robson running around the front of the house and under the porch. Momentarily, Posie arrived and helped a stunned Eddie crawl back out of the garbage can. Eggs oozed from the seams of the egg container.

No one said anything to Eddie as he walked woosily into the kitchen. Anger showed in his face and hands as he spoke. His hands cut the air like two swords. "I've got a headache. I'm going to lie down. Everybody just leave me alone."

For most of the morning everyone pretty much did leave Eddie alone. Nina came in a couple times and tried to find out what had happened outside. Wes came in once to see if Eddie needed something for his headache, and Posie brought him an eggless breakfast. Aside from that, Eddie lay on his sleeping bag and thought about home and Kyle and the skating pond. He pictured his teacher and classmates. He missed them already.

Around noon, the pounding of the headache reduced itself to a throbbing. Eddie was getting hungry for lunch. Quietly moving into the kitchen, he found Gray Eyes there folding some laundry he had brought along. Neither said a word to the other, but Eddie could feel his great-grandfather's eyes on him when he wasn't looking.

Eddie quickly devoured his bowl of soup and watched Gray Eyes, who had finished his laundry and was sitting quietly with his eyes closed. Eddie studied the lines in his great-grandfather's face—the way they curved around his mouth and the deep crow's feet round the eyes. Then suddenly the eyes opened, which startled Eddie.

Gray Eyes stood and said sternly, "Follow me." He led Eddie out onto the back step. When the door was firmly shut he turned to Eddie and said firmly, "the rooster is under the front porch. You have a task."

Chapter 10

Eddie looked up into the serious gaze of his great-grandfather. The old man stepped back as if he were sizing up Eddie. "Wait here," he ordered and walked across to the edge of the woods and came back with a long tree branch. Gray Eyes took the long stout pine branch and snapped it over his knee into the length of a baseball bat. He studied the stick for a moment, nodded and handed it to Eddie.

"What am I supposed to do with this?"

"Your enemy waits under the front porch. Go through the house, out the front door and draw him out. Go face your fear." Gray Eyes pulled open the back door and motioned with his head for Eddie to enter.

Eddie froze and stared at the stick in his hand. There was authority in the old man's voice and it gave Eddie confidence. Yes, he could lick that chicken. He thought that a man that old must know a lot about things like how to get the upper hand on a chicken.

Leaving his great-grandfather at the back step, Eddie slowly moved through the kitchen past the gurgling refrigerator and the black iron stove. Images of the ranting rooster charging after him from under the porch began to erode Eddie's new found confidence. Eddie felt the growing fear extend from the pit of his stomach all the way to his fingertips and into the stick.

Eddie moved down the short hallway, which led past the little living room and on to the front door. He tried moving quickly past the living room door where the grown-ups and Nina were gathered.

Just as Eddie slipped past the doorway, he heard the sharp tones of Phoebe's voice. "Hey there!" Then she said something else Eddie didn't hear.

Hiding the stick behind his leg, Eddie answered, "What? I didn't do anything."

"What's that stick you're hiding?" she inquired crossly and pointed to the hidden stick.

Eddie hesitated a moment while he thought. He pulled the stick up to his shoulder, tilted his head and looked down the length of the stick. "Oh, this? This is just my gun, Phoebe. See? Just playing. Just playing hunting."

"Can I play too?" Nina pleaded hopping off her chair.

"Nope, not this time. I wanna play by myself for a while. Later we'll play."

Eddie turned from his pouting sister and continued down the short hall to the front door, wishing the hall were longer. His heart beat steadily and hard like the Ojibwe pow wow drums he'd heard the night before.

Peering through the storm door Eddie looked left. Then right. Nothing. Softly, he moved through the doorway and across the squeaky boards of the porch. He moved own the steps, ever so slowly. Gripping the stick tighter Eddie stepped out onto the squishy grass. His breathing had quickened. His hand squeezed the stick so tightly, his forearm began to ache.

Suddenly, from beneath the front porch it came. Ten pounds of red fury and terror rushing upon him. Even though he was expecting it, Eddie still jumped clear off the ground. His eyes grew as big as late winter moons and he turned to run. But, before he took the first step, Eddie remembered the nod of Gray Eyes when he'd handed him the stick. There was no time to run anyway. Instantly, Eddie spun around, planted his feet under him, cocked the stick behind his head and gritted his teeth for the onslaught.

Swinging as mightily as he could manage, Eddie missed the bird completely. His momentum, spinning him half way around allowed Robson to jab its beak into Eddie's ankle.

At that moment, some anger trigger was pulled inside Eddie. He didn't feel like running anymore. He suddenly felt stronger and more fearless than he'd ever felt in his life.

With the second swing Eddie struck a blow to the rooster right along side its head. The bird squawked and rolled over twice before shakily returning to its feet. All Eddie's feelings of fear and retreat and all the frustration from being forced to move came forward. Eyes narrowed and jaw set, Eddie rushed the bird again. This strike sent the rooster sprawling and squawking. Feathers floated through the air like oversized spring snowflakes. Eddie taunted the bird. "How do you like that, you big red bag of feathers?"

Robson, got up stunned, looked things over and headed wobbly toward the safety of the woods. Lunging forward after the fleeing bird, Eddie missed his next swing so badly that he lost his balance. Eddie fell flat on his back onto the thawing turf. As quickly as he fell, Eddie got up on one knee and pulled the stick behind his head to fling at the retreating rooster.

Before his arm could come forward with the throw, a hand firmly grabbed the stick from behind. Eddie spun around to see the stern face of his great-grandfather. The old man's serious expression dissolved. Gray Eyes began to laugh. He laughed until he dropped the stick and had to lean over on his knees. He laughed so long and so hard that little tears began to form and run down his cheeks."

"Great-grandfather, are you okay?" asked a confused Eddie.

Gray Eyes held up his index finger to signal to Eddie he was okay, but needed a minute to catch his breath. Once he stopped laughing, the old man said, "I meant for you to smack him one. I didn't mean for you to kill him." Then he started laughing all over again. Eddie had never seen an old person laugh so hard.

And then, for the first time since he left home, Eddie began to laugh. They bent over together laughing. "Did you see that rooster take off?" Eddie howled, pointing toward the woods.

The rooster, now well out of reach, perched himself on a tamarack stump at the edge of the woods. Head cocked to one side, he watched the curious twosome and listened to the strange sounds of human laughter. The bird also heard the front door fly open and fast footsteps clicking across the planking on the porch and then squishing across the soft spring sod. She came down on them like a spring blizzard without warning. After picking up the stick, Phoebe grabbed Eddie's ear lobe and gave it a good tug so that it turned him clear around. Then, for emphasis, she pulled up on his ear so that Eddie stood up on his toes.

"Oweee!" he cried. Because of the pulling on his ear, Eddie's hearing aid worked loose and started to feed back so a high-pitched squealing sound came from Eddie's aid.

Phoebe paid no attention. "How dare you hurt my Robson! That there's a prize winning rooster, and you nearly killed him. I ought to wallop you with this stick." She motioned like she was going to smack Eddie on the leg. "Why, do you have any idea how much a bird like that is worth? What do you got to say for yourself?"

"Let go of my ear. My hearing aid's feeding back. I've got to fix it!"

Phoebe frowned. "I don't know nothing about no hearing aids. Here! Go ahead and fix it. But I ain't going nowhere. What do you got to say? I'm listening." Eddie quickly repositioned the earmold so it fit snugly in his ear.

"Phoebe," he cried, "that rooster's been chasing me and pecking me all the time and scratching me and. . . and I couldn't take it any more. I hate that bird and if I. . . "

Shaking a finger in Eddie's face, she cut him off. "If you ever take after Robson again, I'll take after you, and you'll be sore and sorry." Turning abruptly she stomped off toward the house. Without looking, Phoebe flung the stick out across the yard and unknowingly, almost hit the precious Robson, still perched atop the stump. The bird squawked and ran deeper into the woods.

Eddie's wet angry eyes stared arrows at Phoebe's back as she stomped back to the house. Then he turned toward Gray Eyes, who was about to say something. Eddie narrowed his eyes at the man. "Thanks a lot for nothing, Great-grandfather," he said coldly. Eddie ran around to the back of the house,went in the back door, and marched into his room.

"I'm out of here!" Eddie muttered to himself. He grabbed his backpack and stuffed in some underwear, socks, a map he'd sneaked from the station wagon, and extra batteries for his hearing aid. He turned to head toward the door where he found Nina standing in the doorway.

"Where are you going?"

"Home."

"By yourself?"

"Yep."

"What about Leonard? You can't go without Leonard."

"Leonard's not going. Do you want to come?"

Nina didn't answer right away. "Leonard's not coming? I don't know." She stared at the floor for a moment. "Eddie, we can't go home anyway. Mom and Dad wouldn't let us. We gotta live up here now."

"No, we don't. I don't care what anybody says. I can't stand it here. It's a bad dream. A bunch of mean Phoebes and dirt roads and animals you got to beat off with a stick. And those are supposed to be the tame animals."

"We can't get to Minneapolis from here."

"Yes, we can. We can get anywhere from here. I've got a map. See?" he said waving the map back and forth. "You just got to keep going, and when you get there, you stop."

"You're crazy. How'll we get there? It took us better than four hours to drive here, and we even made a couple wrong turns."

"Take a bus," said Eddie tying the drawstring on his scarlet backpack. I saw busses on the highway coming the other way when we were driving up here. The word 'Minneapolis' was printed in big red letters right above the windshield. I'm just going to catch a ride on one of those." He swung the backpack over one shoulder.

The expression on Nina's face fell. "You can't go. Who'll I play with? Leonard's too old, and it looks like he's got a new girlfriend anyhow. I'm going to be stuck out here with no one to play with."

Eddie could see the idea scared Nina. Tears

spilled out of the corners of her black eyes.

"You can't go, Eddie. I'll tell on you. That's what I'll do." Nina stuck her head into the hallway. "Mom!"

Eddie clapped his hand quickly over her mouth. "Shush up!" Eddie pursed his lips and thought for a moment. "Tell you what. How about you come with me?"

Nina frowned. "Leave Mom and Dad? I don't think I could do that. That's running away from home."

Eddie shook his head. "The way I see it, I'm running away to home. They're the ones that left. They can follow us there if they want to. Who knows? Maybe Mom and Dad can't stand being away from us and they'll come home. I bet they will."

"Well, let's say I did come with you. How much does it cost to take a bus to Minneapolis?"

"I figure it couldn't cost more than about two dollars a person. The busses in the city cost seventy five cents for kids and look at all the traffic they have to drive in. Out here it's easy to drive. There's nobody on the road except for a pick-up truck every ten minutes or so. That should make it cheaper. But then they got more gas to pay for, so that would make it cost a little more. So about two bucks. Three tops."

Nina nodded at her brother. "How much you got?"

"Ten."

"That's more money than I've got, but that's not much money," said Nina.

"It's enough to get us back to Minneapolis. Then we can move in with Kyle. His mom said I can come back and visit anytime. So, you coming? I'm leaving."

Nina said nothing and sat down on the edge of the bed. Eddie stepped past his little sister on his way to the door. Out of the corner of his eye he saw her looking up at him.

She always looks up to me, he thought. After all, he'd been the one who helped feed her and change her when she was little, the one for whom he interpreted when she had her tonsils out and couldn't talk for five days.

"Eddie, even though you're going, I'm not going to miss you."

With a hurt expression on his face, he asked, "How come?"

"Because I'm going too. If you're going, I'm going."

Eddie grinned. "You always did follow me everywhere. Even when you were little and we would be shopping at Sears, you'd even try to follow me into the men's room. Mom had to hold

68

you back, and you'd be screaming and throwing a hissy fit."

Eddie peeked a look out the doorway in the direction of the back door. Turning back to Nina he took a deep breath. "Okay, pack up some stuff and I'll write a note so they'll know where we went."

The quickly written note read:

> Dear Mom and Dad. We
> hate it here. Especially
> me-Eddie. We're going
> home. We're staying with
> Kyle.
> Love,
> Eddie and Nina.

Moments later Nina finished packing and the two slipped out to the kitchen and carefully placed the note under the salt shaker. Grabbing their spring jackets off the wire hooks by the back door, the two peeked outside to be sure they wouldn't be seen. The pair crouched and scooted across the yard toward the woods. Robson had been hiding in the woods since his beating so when he saw Eddie running at him, he squawked and bolted deeper into the woods.

"Now that's a chicken," Eddie said to his

sister as they straightened up and sprinted the last few yards across the clearing. They scurried into a stand of aspen at the edge of the clearing before stopping to look back at the house.

"I guess nobody saw us," said Nina.

"Let's go," said Eddie.

Besides Robson's eyes, one other pair of eyes had followed the children's scampering across the lawn. Gray Eyes looked up at the threatening cloud formations. He shook his head and sighed. I best follow them, he thought to himself and let them learn some things about themselves.

Before the children had gone a half mile into the forest, Nina tapped Eddie on the shoulder. "Excuse me, aren't we going the wrong way? I thought Minneapolis was that way. South." Nina pointed back over her shoulder with her thumb.

"Hey" asked Eddie, "we're Indians aren't we?"

Nina, looking like she wasn't sure what his point was, nodded.

"Well," Eddie continued, "who knows more about the north woods than Indians?"

"Maybe Indians from up here, but we're not from here."

70

"No, but it's in our blood. That's what Dad says, so follow me." Eddie turned to go on.

"Well, I'm not going north to Minneapolis. We'll end up in Canada." Nina folded her arms. "I'm not going to Canada. It's cold up there. Mrs. Lucier said so in social class."

Eddie turned around again. "Okay, okay. I suppose I'll have to tell you. My plan is to go north for a while, cut east and head over to the highway. They'll think we're going south, but we'll be north of Bemidji. Then we can catch one of those busses and head south right through town. See, that way, if they come looking for us, they'll probably be looking south of Bemidji and we'll already be on a bus. Minneapolis, here we come."

"How far are we from the highway?" Nina asked.

"Only about five miles. Or maybe ten. I was watching everything on my way up here while you were sleeping."

"So you know the way?" Nina asked seriously.

"Yeah, no problem. If we just go north and then east to the highway, we can't miss it."

Nina thoughtfully nudged some dried pine needles with her foot and then looked up past the swaying tops of the white pines. "It's clouding up some."

Eddie shrugged his shoulders. "So what? A little snow wouldn't hurt anything. Besides, it's not that cold. Come on, it can't be that much farther."

"I don't know," Nina said haltingly.

"I do know it's not happening back at Grandpa's house," he said bouncing the backpack higher on his back. "If we hurry we can get home in time to shoot some baskets at Kyle's."

"Well," Nina said taking a big breath, "if you think you know the way." Suddenly, Nina spun around. "What was that?"

Eddie shook his head and looked in the same direction as Nina. "I don't see anything. What'd you hear?"

"I heard a snapping sound." Eddie saw her eyes were big with fear. "Eddie, are there bears around here?"

"Naw. Dad always says the bears all live up north."

"Eddie," Nina said, "we are up north. This is up north."

"Oh," Eddie whispered, "I don't think we really have to worry, though. Bears sleep all winter until. . ."

Nina finished her brother's thought, "until spring. This is spring and this is up north. Great."

Grabbing Nina's sleeve, Eddie ran off with his sister. Had Eddie and his sister stopped and looked more closely, they might have seen their great-grandfather crouched behind the tree. They would have found him scolding himself for being so noisy in the woods.

Chapter Eleven

Up and down, the two red backpacks bounced as Eddie and Nina ran recklessly and deeper into the forest. Having run in the general direction of north for ten minutes or so, Eddie and Nina finally stopped to rest. They stood at the top of a hill overlooking a small, pretty lake surrounded by enormous white pines. At one end of the lake stood a lone narrow dock. Other than the dock there were no signs of people around the lake. Panting, Eddie and Nina leaned over with their hands on their knees. Nina swallowed hard and said, "I think we outran it."

"Outran what?" Eddie said straightening up.

"The bear. Why did you think we were running?"

"I wasn't running from anything. I was just running. Just felt like it."

"Eddie, the last time I saw you run like that was the time you smarted off to Abner, that high school kid. He came after you saying he was going to pull your hearing aids out of your ears and stick them up your nose."

"Abner was big," Eddie said.

"So's a bear," Nina added playfully. She lifted her arms up like a giant, her curled fingers the bears paws. She growled, "Raaaaaaargh" and rushed toward Eddie.

"Nina, we don't have time to goof around. We should get moving. Nina. Nina!" He laughed and took a few steps backward. Eddie never saw the football sized rock partly sticking out of the melting snow. Catching his heel, Eddie tumbled backward and right off the top of the steep hill in a series of backward somersaults. After the second revolution Eddie's backpack flew off. During the fourth he was slowed by some brush. He was stopped, finally and solidly, when he slid, back first, into a white pine sapling

By the time Nina scrambled down the bank to her brother, he was sitting up and holding the back of his head. "Eddie, Eddie, are you all right? I'm so sorry. Oh, you're probably going to kill me. Here's your backpack. Oh, what happened to your head? I'm so sorry."

Eddie felt the back of his now sore head. On his hand he found a few drops of bright red blood.

Studying the back of her brother's head , Nina commented, "It's just a little cut, really, but. . ."

Without warning, Eddie quickly reached out, grabbed Nina's ankle and yanked. Down she went with a gasp and a thud. Seeing his sister sitting in the wet snow with such a look of surprise, made Eddie forget his new headache for a moment. "Now we're even," he proclaimed and climbed to his feet. "Now, let's get going."

"What about your head?" Nina signed as she trudged up the embankment ahead of her brother. "Looks to me like you're going to get a big old goose egg on your noggin if you don't put some ice on it."

"Don't worry about it."

"Well, it's my fault. I'll fix up something. Here, turn around now." Reaching into her backpack, Nina pulled out a piece of cloth. She scooped up a pile of cold, grainy, spring snow and folded it into the cloth. Then she reached up and stretched the icy white cloth over Eddie's head. "Now, how's that?"

"Cold, but it does feel pretty good. Thanks." Eddie felt the bandage with his hand. "But Nina, how did you ever think to bring along bandages for this kind of thing? It even has some elastic on it."

"I didn't."

"What do you mean, you didn't? asked Eddie.

"That's not a real bandage. That's a pair of my underpants. Where would I get real bandages?"

Before Nina got the words out of her mouth, Eddie screamed and flung the ice pack off his head. He threw it so hard it helicoptered thirty feet in the air and caught halfway up in a pine tree. There it dangled at the end of a branch. The tree bow slowly bobbed under it's new soggy weight.

"If you ever tell anyone that I had your underwear on my head, I'll. . . I'll. . . I don't know what I'll do. I should just leave you here in the woods," Eddie teased, "and you could just wander around and get lost."

Nina wrinkled her nose at the woods all around them. "That's no big threat because I think we're lost right now."

"We are not," Eddie said.

"Are too."

"Are not."

Eddie stopped to think for a moment, knowing his sister always outlasted him in these ping-pong type arguments. "Tell you what, Nina. First one to knock the underpants off that branch with a snowball is right about us being lost."

"Okay," said Nina excitedly and reached down to pack some snow in her cupped hands. She heaved the snowball and missed.

Eddie followed with a mighty throw which just nicked the underside of the underwear. It swung there for a moment, but didn't fall. After another miss each, Nina connected and blasted the target with an explosion of ice and slush.

"I won, I won!" cried Nina dancing around in victory. "I just knew we were lost. See?" She suddenly frowned at what she had said.

"Fine," said Eddie gathering up their belongings. "So, if you're right, then we're lost. We better get moving."

The two headed deeper into the woods, sloshing their way over the melting snow.

The quiet feet of Gray Eyes padded after them. He paused and studied the children's tracks at each spot the children had stopped. He knew the signs of the forest, especially tracks—the depth and shape of them as well as the meaning of the distances between them. He chuckled at the place where Eddie had fallen down the hill and scraped his head. He wondered how two people, who meandered so widely through the woods could actually be relatives of his.

Very little escaped his gray eyes. He watched the chickadees bobbing and flitting among the branches. All winter, the tiny bird with its black cap, had muttered its one note song: dee-dee, dee-dee. He knew once again he wouldn't be hearing the springtime change in the song. When he used to hear at one hundred percent he always listened for the change. The chickadee's song changed during the spring to a two note song in which the second note drops down and sounds more like: fee-bee, fee-bee.

Gray Eye's momentary sadness disappeared when he caught sight of the first black crow light onto a branch half way up a jack pine. He knew by the bird's arrival that it was time. It had signaled the time for the spring move for generations of his people. Not many were interested any more, though, he thought to himself.

The old man's attention shifted back to the changing sky and the smell of the air. Above a stand of tamaracks, a band of low, slate colored clouds tip-toed in from the southwest. They gave little warning to the untrained eye as to just what was coming. Gray Eyes picked up his pace.

Chapter 12

After a half hour of silent walking, Nina tapped her brother on the shoulder. "Eddie," she signed when he turned around, "how do you know we're heading in the right direction?" Nina pulled her jacket zipper to her chin. "Don't we need a compass or something? It's not like we're in Minneapolis where the streets are all going north-south or east-west."

"I just know in my head," he said tapping his forehead. "My head is like a compass."

"That makes me nervous because your compass has a big old goose egg on the back of it. It could be out of order. Besides, don't we turn east pretty soon? It seems like we've been going north about long enough."

Feeling forced to make a decision, Eddie pointed up ahead. "I figure we turn left up there at that next rise."

"You mean right, don't you?"

"No."

Nina blinked twice and repeated, "You mean right. We turn right, don't we?"

"No."

"Wait a second. If you go north, you turn right to go east, don't you?"

"No way. I looked at a map."

Nina thought for a few moments. "Are you sure you weren't holding the map upside down or something?"

"What difference does that make?"

"Eddie, it doesn't unless you're planning to go to North Dakota instead of home."

"Nina, you worry too much."

"Eddie, you don't worry enough."

Eddie stepped aside and bowed to his sister. "Fine. So you lead, Miss Professional-Map-Reader-of-the-Universe."

Nina took a deep breath and smiled. "Thank you. Well, first, it's supposed to be Ms., not Miss and second, I don't want to lead, really. I just don't want to follow someone who's leading me in the wrong direction."

"Don't worry. We'll be fine. We'll just follow in our stinks."

Nina frowned. She knew Eddie sometimes mixed words and expressions. It came with the territory because Eddie didn't hear as well as other children. "What did you say?" she asked politely.

"In our stinks," Eddie said smartly. "That's what Dad says. We Indians have always followed in our stinks. That's why we're so good at being in the out-of-doors. We just know what to do and we do it."

A light seemed to go on in Nina's head and

it showed through to her face. "Do you mean instincts. Like we follow our instincts?"

"Yeah," replied Eddie. "That's what I said."

"Eddie, we can argue about it later, but if your instincts say go left then we've got a problem." Nina pleaded, "Let's go right. Please? If we go right, I'll pay for the bus tickets. I've got five bucks I wasn't telling you about."

Eddie thought hard for a moment. "I really don't see what the big deal is if the map is upside down. East is east. But, if it means that much to you, I suppose we can go your way."

"Okay," Nina said, trying not to sound too relieved. "Hang a right and let's get going. It's getting colder."

"Yeah, it is," said Eddie scrunching his shoulders up next to his neck. "Let's run for a while. We'll stay warmer."

The children's noisy steps scared up some of the chickadees from their low pine branches. A scarlet-headed Downey woodpecker stopped his inspection of some dead branches in his search for insects. Alarmed gray squirrels side-stepped around to the back sides of their respective trees. And having just arrived from their winter homes were clusters of the tiny, charcoal-gray juncos. Startled by the noisy intruders they scattered and disappeared against a same-colored sky.

At the top of an especially high rise, Nina and Eddie stopped to catch their breath. Round puffs of mist spread out from their mouths like balloons in the Sunday comics. From their vantage point they could see the tree tops and sky for miles in every direction.

"I don't see the highway," said Nina squinting her eyes at the horizon. Eddie's eyes searched too. Nothing.

The wind began to pick up causing the blue and green tops of the pines to sway and roll in wider and wider swirls. The birds and squirrels could no longer be heard against the swishing sounds of the great trees. It was as if the trees had hushed the animals and told them to stop and listen for what was coming. "I hope we're going in the right direction," she said stepping closer to her brother.

Turning his eyes toward the sky, Eddie frowned. "It does look like it's going to rain or snow or something. I think it's getting darker."

"The sky looks weird," Nina added, "but I've never seen this much sky at one time before. It's kind of scary, but it's kind of neat, too. Those clouds over there are rolling in slow motion. And look, over there. It looks like those clouds are sitting down right on top of the trees."

The mid-afternoon sun, glinting through a momentary crack in the clouds, shone on the tops of thousands of acres of evergreen giants. "Wow!" shouted Eddie above the rising sound of the wind. "It looks like the floodlights at the YMCA Christmas tree lot—only a whole lot bigger."

"Lookit!," said Nina pointing toward her right. "Look how shiny it is over there. What's that?"

Eddie gritted his teeth. "Shoot. It's snow. It's snowing over there and it's coming this way."

Suddenly, as Eddie spoke, the sun cut out as if someone had turned off a giant light switch. "Let's hurry up before it gets here." Eddie pulled his hands from his jacket pockets and cupped them over his ears. "The highway must be pretty close. We must have gone five miles by now. I'll bet we just can't see the highway from here because all the trees are in the way."

"Maybe we should go back," Nina said, looking up at Eddie. "We should go back to Grandpa's."

For a few moments Eddie hesitated. He looked around at the darkening forest, the low clouds and the ground they had just covered. "We should get somewhere," he said mostly to himself. Turning to Nina he said, "We're probably closer to the highway than we are to the house now. Let's keep going."

The two ran off again as the first flakes weaved their way through the fabric of evergreen needles and fell to the earth around them.

Having completed a few roller coaster sprints up and down the forest hills, Eddie looked back. To his surprise the clouds had been following them like some enormous gray hounds nipping at their heels. Off they ran again, as if they could somehow outrun the storm and make it tire of it's chase.

On they went, weaving and bobbing through the trunks and under the branches like frantic players in some peculiar football game. The storm's offense grew more intense as they ran. It quickly built up layers of snow on the turf where they cut and slashed around brush and muscular tree limbs.

Panting and sweating after twenty minutes of running, Eddie and Nina climbed and slipped their way to the top of yet one more hill. They suddenly stopped, their heads enveloped in their own breath mist. What they saw filled them with dread. They stared at the sight down the hill behind the tops of the whitening pines. It was a lake with a lone narrow dock at one end. It was a lake where a few drops of Eddie's blood from his recent head wound lay next to a tree. Everything, along with the motionless Nina and Eddie, was quickly and thoroughly being covered with a wind-blown, face-stinging, March blizzard.

Chapter Thirteen

Eddy and Nina were so stunned by the fact they had gone in one huge circle that for several moments they didn't move except for the puffing and blowing of their breathing. The increasing wind penetrated their damp, light jackets and chilled them thoroughly. The driven snow dashed against their exposed skin and smarted their faces and hands.

"Eddie," Nina shouted desperately over the sound of the wind in the trees, "what are we going to do?"

Moving his hands from his ears to his armpits he looked at his sister and shook his head like he didn't hear.

"What should we do?" Nina signed with stiffening fingers.

Eddie looked around at the storm swirling about them and then at his sister. He slowly shook his head. This time Nina took it to mean, "I don't know."

Eddie could see that his sister was beginning to shiver. She wrapped her arms around herself and tucked her chin down. Eddie grabbed his sister by the arm and pulled her back from the edge of the hill. To shelter her, he squatted down and dragged his sister along with himself under the low, flailing branches of a white pine. It looked to Eddie like his sister was losing color from her face. Wrapping his arms around her, he tried to share what little heat he had with Nina.

Huddled against the trunk of the great pine, Eddie tried to think of warmer happier times. He remembered the last time he had held his little sister . It was when she was a toddler. On some of the nights when both of their parents were working and Leonard was busy with something else, he and Nina would sit upstairs before the little upstairs bedroom window. They liked to watch the soft snow fall onto busy Franklin Avenue. Eddie would point out the cars with their gray tire tracks on the new white snow and the people trying to keep their balance on slippery sidewalks. Sometimes he'd sing her little songs he'd learned in school. She never seemed to mind that the melodies weren't right. He'd sing, "I'm a little teapot short and stout. Here is my handle, here is my spout. La la la la la la la la la-he never remembered the next words—Tip me over and pour me out.

Turning to his shivering sister, he rubbed his hand in a circular motion over his chest several times. "I'm sorry Nina. This was my idea. I'm sorry." He squeezed his eyes shut as if trying to shut out the bad dream around him. Nina continued to shiver wildly in his arms and it seemed to be spreading to his own body. He wanted to cry, but he was too cold. Some memorized childhood prayers came to mind and calmed him some, but the shivering continued.

Eddie pulled his attention deep inside, away from the cold and furious storm. Far, far inside he knew there must be a place in him still warm and not shaking. He tried with all his might to find it. With closed eyes he became very still, stiller than he'd ever been before. Then, for a few moments, he found it. There was no storm in that place and no cold and no roosters and no ear pulling Phoebes. And he whispered to that spot and at the same time he seemed to be whispering from that spot. "Help us. Help us. God, please help us."

Suddenly a blast of wind and snow jarred the tree above them. Then immediately, there was a loud screech and he thought he saw the black silhouette of some large bird. The sound cut through the storm and into Eddie's quiet place. He forced himself to open his eyes and then blinked several times because he couldn't believe what he saw. Before them, just below the flailing tree branches, he saw a pair of legs. The pants were baggy, the boots worn. The person knelt down and looked at them shivering against the tree trunk. Too cold to move or be frightened, the children fixed their gaze on Gray Eyes. The face held the expression of both real concern and yet mild amusement. Quickly sizing up the children's condition, Gray Eyes quickly crawled under the tree and wrapped Nina in his coat. "Come. Come with me," he ordered pulling the children from under the tree.

The children stumbled along clinging to their great-grandfather, just barely aware of the swirling nightmare about them. After what seemed like hours they were dragged into a building of some kind. Gray Eyes left them on the floor, stopped for a while to catch his breath, and then quickly slipped back out into the storm. The children soon became dimly aware of sounds like rumblings and clunkings and clanking of metal. Neither heard the small chipping sound of a match being struck or smelled the sulfury aroma of a just-lit match.

The small flame moved from the match and reproduced itself onto the yellowed newspaper and then the logs that sat in the belly of an ugly iron stove. The flames slowly grew. The stove looked as if it was made from a rusty old barrel tipped on it's side. In the end of the barrel was cut a small door for feeding logs to the fire. As the flames grew and glowed Gray Eyes slid the children closer to the stove. "Get those wet things off. They're keeping you cold. It's a good thing for you the crow returned. He showed me where you were. You are very lucky."

The old man hung the wet clothes over a rope that extended across the room and over the stove. Then Gray Eyes dragged a piece of plywood that had been leaning against one of the walls inside the cabin. He propped it up behind Nina and Eddie with a couple old chairs. The barrier focused the heat down on Nina and Eddie.

Ever so gradually, their shivering slowed as the room warmed around them. Gray Eyes brought in some fresh snow in an old coffee can and set it on top of the stove until it melted and then heated to a boil. To this he added something from a pouch he wore around his waist. Pouring the beverage into two cups he said, "Drink," and handed the cups to the children.

The children, now slightly warmer, looked at the brew, then at each other and then back at their great-grandfather.

"Drink this," he repeated pointing at the cups. "You'll feel better."

Through his chattering teeth, Eddie said, "Great-grandfather, it smells like Christmas trees."

"Drink. It will warm you."

Eddie brought the cup to his lips and sipped some of the concoction. Holding the liquid in his mouth, he motioned for Nina to try hers, all the time trying to decide if he should swallow the stuff. Reluctantly, Nina sipped some of the tea and held it in her mouth.

"Swallow now," Gray Eyes ordered. "It's good for you." Eddie took a sip also and held it in his mouth.

"Wha- i- it?" Nina asked while pointing to her mouth.

"It's just water and . . ." Gray Eyes leaned forward and whispered the other ingredient into Nina's ear. Nina immediately spit out the tea in a burst that exploded with a sharp sizzle on the hot barrel stove.

The scene struck Eddie as being so funny that he couldn't hold in his laughter, and he too spit the tea onto the stove. "Great-grandfather, don't you have some hot chocolate or something?"

Gray Eyes, either unable to hear or unwilling to listen to the question, instead ordered, "Drink again. This time swallow it. It won't hurt you. I promise." There was a sternness and ring of authority in his manner and voice, so the children dared not refuse. Obediently, each took a few swallows of the brew, trying not to gag.

After a few moments, they were both pleasantly surprised. A new warmth seemed to radiate out from their stomachs to their chests and out into their limbs. In a half hour they were feeling much like themselves again.

Eddie surveyed the inside of the cabin. "Great-grandfather, what is this place? Whose cabin is it?"

Gray Eyes didn't get the question and asked Eddie to repeat it. Pointing his finger around the cabin, Eddie again asked his questions.

The old man nodded and paused for a moment. Then he began, "For hundreds of years this spot was used by the people for the spring mapling camps. They called these places the sugar bush. Each year after the long hard winters spent in the wigwams that were spread out through the deepest parts of the forest our people,the Anishanabe, would meet here at their sugar bush camps. It was always a happy time. Relatives and friends would meet here after the many months apart and make the maple sugar."

"I thought Dad's side of the family was Ojibwe," said Nina

"We call ourselves the Anishanabe, which means 'first man'. The other tribes call us Ojibwe and the Europeans who came to this area mispronounced Ojibwe and many of their descendants still call us the Chippewa."

"That's a lot of names to remember," said Nina.

"You just have to remember Anishanabe."

"I will, but you should have put some maple sugar in that Anishanabe tea, Great-grandfather," said Eddie pointing to his tea cup.

The old man smiled and looked out the dingy window and through the storm to some long ago time in this same place. "My family was here at this place when I came back from the plains. I had run off, too. Like you two. I went and followed my friend, Nishwa. He was of the Dakota people. He was tall. Most of the Dakota people were tall. We Anishanabe are mostly short and stocky, but strong as bears. Anyway, I followed my friend to his reservation in South Dakota. I spent two years there. My family told me not to go, but I wouldn't listen."

"What did you do there, Great-grandfather?" Nina asked loudly.

"Mostly try to find work. Sometimes I did. Sometimes not. First, I lived at the banks of 'Bear-in-Lodge' Creek near Hisle, but there was little to do. I ran out of money. So then I moved on to the Pine Ridge Reservation. There was some work there fixing roads, but I couldn't stand the open country. It's different from here. The plains

94

there are so open. You see for hundreds of miles towards each of the four winds. And there's no hiding from them and their lonely sounds.

"Here the sparkling white birches, the dark greens of the pines and the golden leaves of the maples in the fall protect you, keep you close and block the winds. A little while ago you were needing shelter. The big pine said to come under her arms. You just knew to do that. The deer do the same thing in a storm. Did you see any?"

Both children shook their heads.

"I know the plains have their own beauty. It was pretty much lost on me. I left there and brought back only three things from the plains." Eddie and Nina waited. "An appreciation of this land, an appreciation of my family and people and this."

Eddie's eyes grew wide as he watched Gray Eyes begin speaking with his hands. The signs were not the same as the signs Eddie learned in school. Excitement shone in Eddie's eyes.

"This is the sign language of the plains Indians," explained Gray Eyes. "There were so many languages with the Dakotas, the Cheyenne, the Pawnee, the Mandan and all the rest—there were over fifty tribes—they needed to find ways to talk to one another. You see, they often met while following the buffalo herds."

95

"Great-grandfather," Nina asked loudly, "how do you say 'thank-you' in your sign language?"

Gray Eyes, with his flat hand facing outward and near his mouth, moved his hand outward and down several times.

"Eddie," said Nina, "that's a lot like our sign for thank-you, isn't it?"

Eddie nodded. Then looking at his Great-grandfather and pointing to himself he said, "This is my sign for thank you." Eddie brought his open right palm, fingers up and in front of his mouth and then brought his hand out and down ending with the palm up.

Gray Eyes imitated the sign.

"What about 'house'?" Nina asked excitedly.

The old man flattened his hands, palms down, and touched the tips of his fingers together so his hands made the shape of a roof.

"Cool! Here's mine," said Eddie.

"Wait," Nina interrupted, "I know it!" She placed both hands in front of her face, palms down, at an angle with fingertips touching and then drew her hands apart and down like she was drawing the roof and sides of a house.

"They are much the same," said Gray Eyes.

The children and Gray Eyes exchanged

signs for the better part of an hour noting that many of the signs were very much alike. Words like see, walk, drink, baby, and sleep were almost the same.

"How about the word 'think'?" Gray Eyes asked with a sly expression.

Both Nina and Eddie quickly pointed to their temples with their index fingers. "Is yours the same, Great-grandfather?" asked Eddie.

"Watch," he said. Taking his index finger Gray Eyes pointed instead to his heart.

"You think with your chest?" asked Nina.

"Not exactly," answered Gray Eyes. "You see the people native to this land believed that thinking comes from the heart, not the brain. It is a big difference. You see our sign for love also is made near the heart. When one thinks and feels together, one makes the right choices. The old man got up to stretch his legs. You see, if your thinking and your love come from the same place, you don't do things like cut an entire forest to the ground or cut huge gashes into Mother Earth's flesh and leave her open like the strip mines over on the Mesabi Range. The minds and hearts of most modern people are not together. It makes them do things like run into the forest without knowing her ways."

"We weren't afraid," Eddie said. "It's just

a woods."

"A healthy fear, no let's say respect for the forest, is not bad. It's okay to go into the forest without a lot of fear, but it's not okay to go into the forest without knowledge."

"Like not knowing how to use a map," Nina added poking Eddie in the ribs.

After the three had a good laugh, Gray Eyes walked over to the window and looked again through the small pane of glass that remained in the mostly boarded window. "What is your sign for mother?" he asked.

With an open right hand, palm facing left, Eddie spread his fingers and with his thumb tapped his chin several times.

Gray Eyes moved from the window. With his bunched hand he touched the left side of his chest. "It too, is over the heart. You see your mother's heart is always with you. You grew inside of her for nine moons just below her heart. For most of the time your heart beat was her heartbeat. The sign for father is near the heart-on the right side, but not so close as the sign for mother."

Eddie frowned. "What are you saying, Great-grandfather?"

"I'm saying that I'd better get back to the house and let your mother and father know that you and your sister are safe." Gray Eyes signaled for Eddie to hand him his jacket.

"We're not going back to that house," declared Eddie.

Gray Eyes looked right at the children. "No, I'll go alone. You'd just slow me down. I don't have time to run from bears that aren't there or attack underclothes with snowballs. There's a storm out there."

"But Great-grandfather," Eddie asked looking nervously out the window, "how'll you make it? I can hardly see out the window."

Gray Eyes waved off the danger. "Bah! I've been through worse storms than this. I know most every tree in this forest. You two put in another log before the fire gets too low. The logs are old, but they're dry. You'll find them under the lean-to along the side the cabin. I'll be back." Pulling the hood up over his long silver head the old man stepped toward the door.

"Wait," Nina said, "are you going to be gone long?"

"Not long," he said pulling open the heavy door. "Have some tea. It will take your mind off the time."

"Great-grandfather, wait!" said Eddie. "How did you ever find us? That's a big woods."

Momentarily closing the door, Gray Eyes

said, "I didn't have to find you. I never really lost you. No, that's not exactly true. I had a little trouble keeping up with you when you ran. But you never went in a straight line anyway. I could see you were starting to circle back. I took a few short cuts. Besides, with the trail you left, it was not hard to follow. A herd of plains buffalo wouldn't have left a much bigger trail." Slowly, Gray Eyes shook his head and smiled to himself. "I was also helped by knowing that I'd better not lose track of you. When you come into the woods knowing so little, sometimes you don't come out. But don't worry about me. I travel with my heart and my thinking in the same place." With that the old man disappeared into the swarming flakes and pulled the door shut behind him.

Chapter 14

An armful of heavy logs tumbled from Eddie's arms and rumbled onto the bare planks of the cabin floor. He rearranged the blanket over his shoulders and kicked off his still wet shoes.

"What if he has a heart attack or something?" Nina asked nervously. " It's been a couple hours."

"Have some tea," Eddie said as he pried open the door of the barrel stove. "I don't know why it's taking so long. Maybe Phoebe got after him for getting me to smack her chicken."

"That's a rooster," corrected Nina. "It's not a chicken. You're supposed to call it a rooster."

"I'd like to call it dinner," he said squinting into a hot stove."

"I'd like to call anything dinner about now," complained Nina. "I'm not having a very good day. So far today I got lost in the woods, then I thought I got chased by a bear. Then I pushed my brother off a small cliff, had my underpants thrown up a tree, almost froze to death in a blizzard . . ."

Eddie held up his hand. "Before I forget, next time it's your turn to get the logs."

"You know Job didn't get any sympathy

either. That's who I feel like."

"Who?"

"Job. He's one of those guys back in the Bible days. His life went from great to awful in one day. He lost his seven thousand sheep to lightning, and then the roof of his house fell in and wiped out his family, and then he got boils all over his body."

"Boy, I'm glad I didn't live back then," said Eddie. "If a guy wasn't getting thrown to the lions, he was getting stoned or flooded or covered with locusts."

"Yeah," agreed Nina, "but the worst would be turning into a salt lady."

"What salt lady?"

Standing up to demonstrate Nina said, "This lady, she was too curious. She looked back at this big city on fire and got turned right into a salt lady. Right in her steps." Nina lifted her leg up and stopped in mid-motion.

"Kind of like frozen tag? And just for being curious?"

"Yeah, but she had been warned."

Nina stood up and opened the door to the stove. The ember glow spread across her face and shoulders. Without their noticing, the room had slowly darkened as the sun set somewhere out beyond the snowy reach of the storm. Outside the thin walls of their shack, the wind howled like some far away timberwolf. Between the gusts, Nina could hear the plinking sound of iced snow flakes against the panes of wet black glass.

"Hey, our clothes are dry," said Eddie pulling his sweatshirt off the line above the stove. "We'll be set for heading the rest of the way home tomorrow. I bet this storm will quit by morning. Then we'll be on our way."

"Sure, but to where?" asked Nina smoothing away the wrinkles of her sweatshirt.

"Home," said Eddie.

"I'm not so sure anymore, Eddie. We should have stayed on the road or something. I don't think we can do it."

"I'll bet Great-grandfather will help us. After all, he followed us into the woods and never squealed on us or stopped us. He was just following us to be sure we didn't get lost or anything."

"Well, we sure didn't disappoint him," Nina said shaking the stiffness from one of her socks.

Presently, the two got as comfortable as they could on the plank floor. With their jackets rolled up for pillows they watched the bounce and flicker of the flames.

Eddie was unable to hear the storm's wolf-like attempts to huff and puff and blow their house down. The new weight of the snow on the roof made the rafters groan.

"Eddie," Nina said and signed to Eddie, "sometimes you're lucky you don't hear so well. It sounds like the roof is going to collapse."

"Don't worry," Eddie said removing his hearing aids for the night. "If this cabin has been here this many years, it'll go one more storm. Just go to sleep."

It seemed like his eyelids had just slipped down when Eddie was stirred by the floor vibrations of someone moving into the room. Heavy wool blankets were wrapped around him and Nina. A cold and aged hand patted him on the head like some sort of blessing, and Eddie tumbled back down into a deep dream-filled sleep.

In Eddie's sleep there were vivid pictures of gray, stinging snow against black skies and cowering trees. There was a dream about Minneapolis where he saw bears in cars and wolves standing on street corners. He saw the skating rink with a girl skating in large lazy loops, her black hair flowing behind her. She skated backward causing her shiny hair to blow over her face covering it except for her eyes. He saw his house in Minneapolis with the warm lights from the kitchen flooding out onto the snowy back yard.

Off and on through the night, Eddie was

pulled from his dream by the reassuring movement of footsteps, and the sound of clunking logs and the metallic sound of the stove door.

Chapter 15

By morning the blizzard had blown east of Bemidji and Duluth and finally exhausted itself over Lake Superior. By nine o'clock the new snow was beginning to melt. Icy-cold, melted water from the cabin's roof dripped steadily off the eaves. The drops fell in neat rows, cutting deep trenches in the two feet of new soft snow. The sun light put a dazzle on it, white and clean as a hospital sink.

Nina was awakened by the sizzling sound of water drops leaking through the roof and instantly frying on the hot barrel stove. Eddie felt the heavy boot steps on the rough wooden floorboards. Sitting up slowly, he rubbed the stiff spots that he got from sleeping on the hard floor and put on his hearing aids,

"Great-grandfather," said Eddie turning around. "What's your sign for morning?"

Gray Eyes shook his head. He hadn't heard.

"Morning," Eddie said loudly and pointed to the window. "Good morning."

Gray Eyes heard this time. With the palm of his right hand down he formed a circle with his thumb and index finger so together they looked like a little sun. He then lifted the little sun up in the air about a foot.

Eddie and Nina copied the movement several times.

"What is your sign for morning?" asked Gray Eyes.

"Can I do it?" Nina asked. With both hands open Nina extended her right hand out with her palm up. Then she placed the finger tips of her left hand in the crook of her right elbow. Next she bent her right arm at the elbow bringing the right hand up toward her face.

"Not so different," their great-grandfather said as he copied the sign a few times.

"Great-grandfather," said Nina with a pained look on her face. "I need to know a sign for bathroom. I really need to go."

Smiling, Gray Eyes held out his left hand about ten inches in front of his shoulder with fingers spread. The back of the hand faced outward. He slowly moved the hand upward.

"That's the sign for bathroom?" asked Nina.

"That's the Indian sign for woods," laughed Gray Eyes.

"Oh," said Nina and took a roll of tissue paper from Gray Eyes.

"Lot's of trees. No waiting," joked Eddie as Nina headed toward the door.

"Or you could use the outhouse," said Gray Eyes stoking the fire. "It's behind the cabin. No one's been in there for a couple years. Open the door carefully. Could be something living in there."

Nina looked at her brother with pleading eyes.

"Okay, okay," complained Eddie. "I'll come and check it for you first."

Once outside the cabin Eddie saw what the area looked like in daylight without a storm hiding it. The cabin was set in a small clearing surrounded by a huge stand of some kind of tree. They were not the needle bearing type of tree, but tall branching trees, some a hundred feet tall with smooth, squirrel-gray bark.

Nina's mind was on other things. "Come on," she said tugging at Eddie's sleeve. "I want to ask you something as we walk. Are you sure we should keep going? I don't think Great-grandfather is going to let us go to Minneapolis."

"Didn't you hear him? He ran off when he was a kid. All the way to South Dakota, too. He should understand."

"I don't know about that," Nina said. "But I do know I gotta go." Ever so slowly, Nina opened the door of the outhouse. Peeking around the corner of the door she barked like a dog.

"Rarf! Rarf! Rarf!"

"What are you doing?" laughed Eddie pulling the door open. "There's nothing in there. Great-grandfather was just kidding."

Just then a chipmunk tore out of the outhouse and scampered right over Eddie's feet. Startled, Eddie jumped and remained in the air for what seemed like ten seconds. When he finally came down, his feet slipped out from under him and he sat down with a plop right on the wet snow.

Nina stepped in through the doorway. "Gee, thanks for protecting me, big brother," she said smartly and closed the outhouse door behind her.

On their return trip from the outhouse, Eddie outlined his plan for Nina. "Okay, we have a little breakfast, talk for a while, help clean up, ask for directions, some extra food, say thank-you and off we go."

"I miss Mom and Dad and Leonard," said Nina looking down at her tracks in the snow. "Don't you?"

"Yeah, but that will only be until they move back home. If we go, I know they'll come. See, I want Mom and Dad and Leonard there and Kyle and my other friends and my teacher, Cheryl. I don't know where I'd be without her. Well, yes I do. I'd be here in Bemidji trying to get back to

Minneapolis."

As Eddie and Nina were about to enter the cabin Nina pointed. "Look at all that stuff." Stacked on an old toboggan were several piles of buckets, some big jugs, and some khaki colored sacks filled with lumpy things. "What are all these buckets for?" Nina asked. "Are we supposed to clean this place or something?"

Eddie shrugged and opened the door. Back inside Gray Eyes was bent over the barrel stove frying up some eggs and bacon on a black iron skillet.

"How do you like your eggs?"

"Over hard, I guess," answered Eddie.

"You have to speak up," said Gray Eyes impatiently.

"Over hard," Eddie repeated, but this time as he spoke he tapped his fists together.

"Over easy," Nina said loudly.

Skillfully, Gray Eyes maneuvered the big flat bottomed skillet on the round top of the stove. "The eggs pretty much turn out sunny side up and crispy. I like to ask just the same. You'll need to eat well. We've got work to do today. So how many eggs do you each want?"

"Ah, two," Eddie answered. "But Great-grandfather, ah, we have to be going. We don't have time to stay and work. We thought you might point out the way to the highway and . . ."

Shaking his head, the old man said, "First work and then I'll show you the way. There is much work to be done, and I can't do it alone. The trees are ready."

"How long is this going to take?" Eddie looked at his sister. "We could spare maybe an hour or two. How long do you need us?"

"Four or five," Gray Eyes answered.

"Four or five hours?" Eddie groaned. "That'll shoot most of the day."

"No," frowned the old man, "Four or five days. Maybe as many as six or seven, but that would be the most."

The mouths of both children dropped open. "What's there to do here that takes so long?" Eddie asked. "Are we going to cut down the whole North Woods?"

"I'm too little to cut down trees," complained Nina. "Besides, I like trees."

"Does it have something to do with the buckets outside?" Eddie asked.

"Now you're getting warm, but your bacon is getting burnt. Here eat up."

Eddie scurried to the back side of the stove to get Gray Eye's attention. "We can't stay. We've got to be going!"

"Four or five days are nothing. When

you're my age, four or five days seems like a few hours."

"But to kids it seems like four or five years!" protested Eddie.

"When you're busy in the forest there will be no time. Not for either of us. You'll see."

Nina and Eddie shot sideways glances at each other to see if the other knew what the old man was talking about.

"I don't think so, Great-grandfather. We really gotta go."

Gray Eyes looked up from the sizzling skillet. "You'll never find your way out of the forest. You'll go round and round in circles and starve to death or freeze. The nights are still freezing and the days are warm. That's why we will stay for a while. Then I'll show you the way out. But first we work."

Chapter 16

"Here," said Gray Eyes dumping the contents of a large canvas bag onto the cabin floor, "put these rubber knee boots on. You'll need them." Along with the boots, out tumbled a pair of wooden mallets, two, old, hand-operated drills, and dozens of short pieces of tubing.

"What's all this stuff for?" asked Nina.

"Sugar," answered Gray Eyes.

"Sugar?" asked Eddie. "What do drills have to do with sugar?"

"Maple sugar. Not that white stuff. We're going to make our own from the maple trees like our people have done in these forests for thousands of years."

"Cool!" said Nina reaching for a pair of boots. "Eddie, we're going to get sugar from those trees outside!"

"Let's go," said Gray Eyes waving the children toward the door. "It's the right time. The days are warm—above freezing and the nights are crisp and cold. It sets the sap flowing up the trunk."

"But why are we going to all this trouble?" complained Eddie. "Isn't it a lot easier to buy some sugar at the store. I mean a whole week, just to get some sugar?"

"There are three reasons," said Gray Eyes leading the children out the door and into the bright sunlight. "One reason is that it's maple sugar, which is the best sweetener in the world, and another is that it's a way for some of us to make some money. The third reason is that it's a tradition of the Anishanabe people.

"Every spring after the long winter the people came from their separate places in the forests. They would meet in the sugar camps. It was a time of great joy. Friends and relatives, who hadn't seen each other all winter, were rejoined."

"Did they stay in this cabin?" asked Nina.

Gray Eyes pointed to his ear.

Nina repeated her question.

"The people lived in bark houses. The frames were left here all year, but they rolled up the birch bark and carried it with them to the summer camp. See, the Anishanabe—the Ojibwe people and the Dakota people before them, lived one season at each of four camps. In the summer they lived next to the cooling blue lakes where they could fish and swim and bathe. In the fall they moved to the wild rice paddies. There, they took the canoes out to gather the wild rice from the shallow water of lakes and rivers. In the winter they lived in skin houses spread out in the shelter

114

of the deep forest away from the winds. Then, in the spring they'd come here.

"I can still see myself in this clearing of maples when I was a boy. Back then the old people called the trees 'a nina tig'. It was before I was sent to the mission school. My family all wore their hair long. How it glistened in the spring sun. We little boys ran and hunted small birds— and sometimes each other with our little bows and blunt arrows. The girls, always with their mothers, learned the many skills of the Anishanabe women. If I close my eyes they are still here with their brightly colored crafts, their endless chores, their songs and stories. Over there the huge brass kettle, the 'akik', hung from a branch over the fire in the center of the camp. It had been bought from a French trader at the trading post at Duluth. A pile of beaver pelts as high as a man had been the cost. Spread around here were the white, birch covered lodges. After a spring snow like yesterday the lodges would look like big snow drifts with smoke coming out the tops."

Both Eddie and Nina remained silent looking around the camp, hoping to see some of what their Great-grandfather could see. Suddenly, Gray Eyes clapped his hands together and pointed to the three stacks of tin buckets. "Here, carry these and follow me," he said, swinging the canvas sack over his shoulder and stepping high through the deep snow.

The children followed as best they could in their great-grandfather's footsteps until they arrived at the base of a large sugar maple. Looking up at the tree and then reaching around the tree as far as he could, Gray Eyes said, "Three taps." Then sliding around the tree a bit he said, "Right here. It's best to tap the tree one and a half to three feet from the ground on the south side of the tree."

Nina looked around her. "How do you know which way is south? I don't see a compass or anything."

"There are signs if you know what to look for. The sun came up over those trees this morning. So that must be east and that must be south over there. Also, you can tell by the snow melting. It melts faster on the south side of the tree. This afternoon when the snow gets to melting, you'll see it. Another way of finding south is to look at which side of the tree the moss grows on. Moss grows better on the north side of the tree where it is shadier. The opposite side of the tree is facing south."

Nina and Eddie walked around several trees looking for moss. "Yeah," said Eddie. "The moss is on the same side of the trees."

116

"Now, back to drilling. It's better, too, if the hole, the 'oji guigan' is under a big branch."

After checking overhead for a large branch, Gray Eyes dug in the bag and pulled out two hand drills. Handing one to Eddie, he said, "Watch." Squatting down, the old man pressed the drill bit against the soft bark. At an upward angle he drilled until the bit had gone about three inches into the trunk. Withdrawing the tool, he used the drill bit to clean the wood shavings from the hole.

"Hand me a 'negwa kwun' and the hammer."

"A what?" asked Eddie.

"A spile. The spout, the little hollow tubes. We need to pound them into the hole so the sap can run out."

With a few taps of the hammer the spile was snugly inserted into the trees. Gray Eyes hung a bucket on the spile and covered it with a special cover to keep out the rain and debris.

"Nothing's happening," said Nina crouching down and looking into the end of the spile.

"You have to be a little patient," said Gray Eyes. "The tree isn't a faucet. It will take some time. Come, let's put in the next spile."

"Wait a second," called Nina. "Look!" A drop of sparkling, water-colored sap rolled off the end of the spile and plopped into the empty bucket.

"You see," Gray Eyes said. "A little patience. Not a lot. Just a little."

The three noisily worked their way through the sunny grove. The sharp sound of tapping hammers on the wooden spiles vibrated up each tree trunk, setting the air around it into sound waves that echoed off the surrounding trees. The sound was punctuated by the hollow metal sound of the tin buckets. Otherwise, the forest was quiet except for the chipping and chirping of small birds, the steady dripping of melting snow and the quiet plop of sap in metal buckets.

Chapter 17

After two hours of drilling and hammering, Gray Eyes signaled that enough trees had been tapped. "Follow me," he said. Eddie and Nina traced their great-grandfather's steps back toward the cabin. But instead of going inside he led them around back to a small lean-to structure that stood only three feet or so from the ground at its highest spot. There was a small door at one end.

"What's in there?" asked Eddie.

"If someone hasn't stolen it, it's something very old. It's been in this maple grove for two hundred years." Gray Eyes kicked snow away from the base of the door and pulled it open.

"Is there a treasure in there?" asked Nina trying to peer into the dark enclosure.

"Today, not many would think this is a treasure. It was a treasure to me and your ancestors at one time, though. Here," Gray Eyes said crawling into the opening, "help me roll this out of here." With much slipping and groaning and gritting of teeth, the trio rolled out a huge brass kettle.

"Wow!" exclaimed Eddie. "That's the biggest pot I've ever seen. What did you cook in there? Whole bears at one time?"

"Whoa!" said Nina. "It looks like a witch

cauldron or like the one the three pigs put under the big bad wolf when he came down the chimney."

"You children watch too much TV," Gray Eyes said pushing the kettle upright. "We've got to get this cleaned up and ready for the sugar."

"We're going to put all the sap in there?" asked Eddie.

"Yes, and we're going to roll it over there and boil the sap."

"What are we going to boil it on? There's no stove or anything."

"I know what I'm doing," said Gray Eyes. "Enough questions. You just help me roll this thing over to that clearing."

Once the kettle was rolled to its destination, Gray Eyes and the children rigged two upright posts from the wood pile. They were placed about ten feet apart. Between these they placed a cross bar that stood about six feet from the ground. With his hatchet Gray Eyes went to work on another branch. He removed all the branches except for a short one left near the end which would act as a hook to hang over the cross bar. At the other end he cut a notch. "The pot's handle fits in here," said Gray Eyes.

For the better part of two hours the three worked cleaning out the inside of the old kettle

120

using soap and wet snow. Sand from a nearby creek was used for scouring. "When I was young, my mother used lye instead of soap. That's all we had. The women had tough hands. Tougher than the men's hands."

"What's lye?" asked Nina looking at her hands. "I never heard of it."

"Lye is a liquid people once used to clean things. The women would take the ashes from hardwood trees like maple and oak. They would boil the ashes in water and then strain out the ashes."

"Seems like a lot of work," Eddie said wrinkling his nose. Then seeing Gray Eyes hadn't heard him he repeated, "Seems like a lot of work!"

"Everybody worked. It was the way people lived. The old people taught the children patience and the discipline to work. Those were the two lessons."

"So the parents were really strict?" Nina asked.

"The children were always taught with gentleness. Children were never spanked. The older people mostly taught by example. But sometimes they might tell the children stories that would frighten them a little so they would do what they were told."

"Like what?" Eddie asked loudly.

Gray Eyes stood up to stretch. "It was important to teach the children to be quiet in the evenings. It was out of respect for the old people, and in earlier times a screaming child could give away the location of the village to an approaching enemy. Of course, this keeping still was a hard thing for us children to do. If we were noisy my mother would say, 'Keep still or the owl will get you.' If we still didn't quiet down she would walk to the door of the wigwam, hold back the blanket and say, 'Come in owl. Come and get these children who won't be still.' We would hide our heads under the blankets and soon be asleep.

"So let's get this pot up on the hook," said Gray Eyes with a twinkle in his eyes, "or I'll have to get the owl after you two."

"But how are we going to get this thing up onto that hook," asked Nina. "We could hardly roll it over here."

"You're right," said Gray Eyes stroking his chin. "It's solid brass." Giving a tug on the handle, he said, "Bah, when I was a young man I could lift that kettle up by myself."

"So, I guess we'll have to skip it this year," Eddie said hopefully.

Gray Eyes never heard Eddie. "We've got to get this pot up and a fire started before the buckets fill up. Follow me." The children trudged after their Great-grandfather to the pile of logs. Pulling out a pair of birch logs about six feet long, Gray Eyes instructed the children to drag them over to the kettle.

Next, the three scraped the surrounding snow into a three foot high pile under the spot where the kettle would hang. "Okay, now lay the two logs about a foot apart with a pair of the ends leaning on the pile."

"Oh, I get it," said Nina, "A ramp."

Eddie had to smile at his great-grandfather's ingenuity.

Once the kettle was in place, the trio kicked out the snow from under the pot. Then they stepped back to admire their work. To Eddie the work represented one less thing to do before leaving for Minneapolis. Looking up at Gray Eyes, Eddie could see the old man was once again seeing the clearing as it had been so many years ago. Then Gray Eyes quickly turned toward the shack. "Let's eat. Then we get to work."

Once inside, Gray Eyes pulled out a big red and white water jug he had brought along on the toboggan. "Fresh water. The snow's not so clean as it used to be. More tea?"

"No thanks," Eddie said quickly. "I'm mostly hungry."

123

From the sack Gray Eyes pulled some cans of soup, cords of beef jerky, some hard cheeses, dry milk, a couple boxes of corn flakes, raw carrots and a few things Eddie did not recognize.

"What's that stuff?" Nina asked pointing to some round, flat, gold-colored food.

"Bread," said Gray Eyes holding up a piece. "Lagolet bread. My mother used to make this many years ago." He handed the bread to Nina.

She felt the bread and handed it to Eddie.

"Wow, it's really hard." Nina said.

"Yeah, are you sure your mother didn't cook this piece of bread?"

Gray Eyes laughed. "Yes, I'm sure. It's supposed to be hard. This was baked by an old woman who lives near me on the reservation. She still makes the Lagolet bread by mixing flour and salt with water and kneads it until it's very hard. Then she bakes it in her oven. My mother never had a real oven so she placed the bread on a stick over the fire. Try some." he said taking the loaf and breaking it in two.

"It could use a little jelly," Eddie said loudly.

"In the sack there's some. Years ago, we would pick berries when they were in season. They would be dried for storage so they wouldn't spoil. Then, whenever we wished for some, they could be brought out and boiled. Sometimes the berries would be mixed with maple sugar and that would be our jelly."

"Sounds good," Nina said yanking off another piece of bread with her teeth. "What kind of berries did you eat?"

Not hearing her, Gray Eyes continued chewing on a piece of Lagolet bread.

"Great-grandfather," Eddie asked loudly. "May I ask you something?"

Gray Eyes nodded.

"Did you ever try wearing a hearing aid?" Eddie pointed to his own hearing aid. "It really helps me a lot. I bet it could make it easier for you to hear stuff."

"Bah," answered Gray Eyes waving off the idea. "I don't want any wires and microphones stuck in my head. I'm alone most of the time, anyway. It's not important. Now, eat your Lagolet bread."

"They really help most people hear better. Lots of old people, I mean, lots of people your age use them."

"There aren't many people my age," commented Gray Eyes mostly to himself. "Eat up. The Lagolet bread will put some flesh on your bones. It will help you work, too."

Chapter 18

Gray Eyes led Eddie and Nina out onto the front step. Turning his face toward the midday sun, he took in a deep breath through his nose. "You can smell the earth again," he said. "The ice is releasing its hold on her." Looking thoughtfully at the children he continued, "To me, there are five signs of spring—one for each sense. Smelling the earth is one; the sighting of the first crow is another; the feeling of warm sun on the skin is a third; the fourth is the taste of maple sugar; and the fifth is the best—the sound of the geese returning."

"Spring must be mostly here then," said Nina, "except for the maple sugar and the geese."

"The maple sugar will take some discipline," explained Gray Eyes, "and waiting for the geese will take some patience. Being good Anishanabe people we have both." He looked at the two faces of his great-grandchildren. Nina smiled up at him, but Eddie's eyes searched the surrounding woods.

Eddie squinted up at the sun and sighed. "Let's get to it," he said. "We've got to be going." Eddie pictured Grey Eyes leading Nina and him through the forest and out to the highway where they could be on their way to Bemidji, and then

126

home to Minneapolis. Then, not long after their arrival, Mom, Dad, and Leonard would show up. They'd be mad at first, but that would be okay. After a little they could pick up their lives where they'd left off.

While Nina went from tree to tree gathering the fresh sap, Eddie began hauling wood from the pile to where Gray Eyes prepared the kindling for the fire. "We will need eight to ten gallons of sap in the kettle before we start boiling. Once the boiling begins, we will be using lots of wood. Keep hauling. Use the toboggan; that's what it's for."

After several loads Eddie stopped to rest. Sitting on the end of a log, he watched his great-grandfather carrying the maple sap to the kettle. He watched Gray Eye's long pony tail swing back and forth as he walked. "Great-grandfather," Eddie said loudly and pointed to his hair, "why do you wear your hair so long? Isn't that kind of old-fashioned?"

"No. Many people still observe it. Like Christmas to the Christians, it's an old practice, but it's meaningful. My father believed he would lose all his strength if his hair was cut. He had a vision when he was a young man. He dreamed that his life was in his hair. When he went to battle against the Dakota, it seemed that the enemy could not see him because of his shining hair. Then, when the fighting cleared up, others could see him again."

"Have you always had long hair Great-grandfather?" asked Eddie loudly.

Pouring the maple sap into the kettle Gray Eyes said, "When I was very young, my mother brought me to the missionary school. The teacher there asked my mother if she could cut my long hair. My mother objected strongly. But when she left, they cut it anyway, saying it was a rule of the school. When my mother came back and saw my hair, she wept and wouldn't be comforted."

"Wow," said Eddie seriously. "Now you could sue the schools. You can wear your hair any way you want to."

"You know," said Gray Eyes, "we have something in common. When I was forced to go to the missionary school, they were very harsh and taught us to abandon our old ways. I ran away from the school to be with my family. You too, are running away, but you are abandoning your family to run back to your school. It seems strange to me."

Eddie grew quiet and went off to get more logs. I'm not running away from anything, he thought. I'm running back home and bringing them all back with me. They're the ones running away from home.

Late that afternoon, the temperature dropped and a blue-gray mass of low clouds drifted in, bringing a light dusting of snow. It covered the ground and masked the muddy tracks they had left that day. With the drop in temperature the sap slowed as did the work. Nina and Eddie watched Gray Eyes carefully stir the sap with a clean canoe paddle.

"You see, when the water is mostly boiled off, the color begins to turn amber."

"Yeah," said Eddie. "It looks kind of like a clear gold."

"Can I try some?" Nina pleaded.

"Here, try some from the paddle. The sugar in the kettle is too hot." Eddie and Nina each ran a finger from the paddle to their mouths.

"Mmm. Sweet," said Nina.

Eddie said nothing, but took another fingerful of the sweet warm syrup.

"It has been a good day," said Gray Eyes looking up at the falling snow. "This may be the last night I can tell you young people the old stories."

"Why?" asked Eddie hopefully. "Are we going tomorrow?"

"No, we've just begun. The maple sugaring takes many days. I must tell you the old stories tonight since they can only be told with snow covering the ground. It is then that the spirits rest in the ground. When the snow melts, the spirits come out. Telling the old stories with the spirits about brings misfortune."

"Oh," said Eddie.

"I love stories," Nina said excitedly. "Tell us one now."

"The snow needs to be deeper. After we eat."

When the dinner of soup and potatoes was finished, Nina and Eddie helped clean up the dishes. Quickly, Eddie and Nina made their beds up near the stove. Eddie watched as Gray Eyes turned from the window. "Turn your beds around. You should always sleep with your feet toward the fire. That's the way it's done." Then motioning toward the window, he said, "Now that the snow is covering the ground I can tell you one of the stories of Winabojo."

"Is he a friend of yours?" asked Nina.

"No," laughed Gray Eyes. "Winabojo is called the Master of Life. He gives life and helps all the animals stay alive by giving them their tricks. The fox is cunning, the bird is fast, the moose is strong. Winabojo taught them these things. He also gave the early people most of their best remedies."

130

"Like tea for keeping warm?" asked Nina.

Gray Eyes didn't hear at first, but nodded and laughed when Eddie repeated Nina's question. "Winabojo was always wandering and walking through the woods. One day after following many streams and gathering berries, he saw a lot of loons diving at the other end of the lake. When the loons

saw Winabojo, they became frightened and began to fly away. Winabojo said, 'Don't go. We are friends.' Then the birds came to him in flocks. 'We will have fun. I will dive too,' he said. He made a bet with the loons that he could stay under the water and swim farther than the loons. Now loons are very skillful swimmers, and they swim under water with their eyes open. But Winabojo had always told the Ojibwe people to swim with their eyes closed. Taking a deep breath, Winabojo threw himself into the water, but since he could not see, he dashed his head against a great rock. It stunned him and cut a gash in his forehead.

"Seeing this, the loons said, 'Winabojo cannot be killed. He is so foolish he will surely blame us. Then he will come and harm us.' Winabojo drifted down stream and awoke from his head injury in some bushes. He took some clay and put it on his forehead to stop the bleeding. After a while he got up and went to his grandmother who could cure him. She scolded him for his heedlessness and cured him with an herb.'

"That story is called, 'Winabojo diving for a wager.' "

"What does 'heedlessness' mean Great-grandfather?"

"It means not being wary. Not being careful. It is like running away into the forest without knowledge."

Neither Eddie nor Nina said anything for a few moments. Finally, Eddie said, "Great-grandfather, show us some more things to say in your sign language."

"You know, it's too bad you are leaving," said Gray Eyes. "The sign language of the plains people is a dying language. Unless some of the old ones pass it on to the young, it will be lost."

Then Gray Eyes held his left hand open, back outward and with the fingers spread pointing upward, he moved them up slightly. "Remember from before? This is the sign for tree." Then pointing his right index finger up, he moved it up and down several times. "This means people. If you put the signs together you have the signs for the Ojibwe people. See? The tree . . . people. We are the people who live among the trees."

Both Eddie and Nina imitated the signs.

"Great-grandfather," said Eddie, "you don't move your face or make any expressions when you talk. I was taught that it helps people understand."

"No, we believe it is all said with the hands. The face should show composure and dignity. Usually, signing was used with strangers from other tribes. One should not use expressions that might betray fear or uneasiness. It may encourage one's enemies."

For the next few days, the three collected and boiled the sap. They traded signs and stories and ate. Though he fought it, Eddie found himself getting into the daily rhythm of working, eating, sharing the songs and stories and sleeping. At first, it was minutes between thoughts of leaving for Minneapolis, then hours.

On the seventh morning, when the three walked out to the boiling place, Gray Eyes said, "Tonight I am going to take a liberty and give you new names."

"Cool," said Nina. "Could I have Tiffany? I don't know why. I just love that name."

Eddie slowly shook his head. "No, he means Ojibwe names. Not names like Tiffany or Judy or Becky."

"Oh," said Nina quietly.

Gray Eyes continued. "It's a custom that a namer gives a child a name. I would like to be your namer. We will talk more of this tonight. For now we have sap to collect."

That night after cleaning the dishes and washing themselves, Eddie and Nina sat near the stove and waited for their Great-grandfather. Sitting in a wooden chair, he pulled up close to them. "There is a ceremony in which the namer shares the name for the child that has been given to him in a dream. I was not there when you were infants, but the night you came to this cabin I had two dreams.

134

"The first dream was for Eddie. In it there was the black crow that flushed up from the pine when you hid from the storm. The crow's wing was curved on one side until it almost made a circle. The bird repeatedly moved its wing from the lower part of its head to the upper part of its head. The crow that day showed me where you were. For our people the crow is the signal of spring, new life, and the time for maple sugaring to begin. I knew you were to stay and learn from our time in the sugar bush. As I followed you through the forest, I could not always keep up with you. I wasn't always sure where you were. The snow began covering your tracks too quickly. But then the crow pointed you out to me or you may have died. Eddie, I give you the name Crow-Above-the-Pines."

The memory of the crow exploding out of the pine tree during the blizzard came back to Eddie. It was just then that his Great-grandfather appeared to save them.

Eddie studied the face of Gray Eyes. What was there about this old man? he thought. The dream of the crow making the sign—how could he know that? It was one of his own signs. He hadn't taught his great-grandfather that one. What did it all mean?

Next, Gray Eyes turned to Nina. "In the

135

other dream a wind came up from the south and spun around me in circles. There was a shock of black hair trailing behind this fast little wind. It came to me that the wind was you. You have a mind that learns fast. You know your brother's signs as well as he. You watch the signs I show you once, and you know them. You move quickly, speak quickly and sign quickly. The name for you is Nodinens."

"What does it mean?" Nina interrupted.

"Nodinens means Little Wind. You move and think like a little wind."

Grinning widely, Nina turned to her brother and made a windy sound with her rounded mouth while blowing on Eddie's face. "Come on, Crow-Above-the-Pines," she said playfully. "Let's hear some crowing sounds."

Eddie narrowed his eyes and slowly unfolded his arms like a pair of wings. "Caw, caw, caw," he called and brought himself to a crouched position. He waved his wings and made stiff short steps around his sleeping bag and then onto the floor. Like the dancers he'd seen at the powwow, Eddie began turning and stepping higher and higher. Around the wood stove he stepped.

Nina watched with big eyes as her brother lost himself in the movement. She too, hopped up and began her own interpretation of her new name. With her arms spread like the blades of a windmill, Nina spun round and round. She twisted around like a poorly trained, yet enthusiastic, ballerina. All the while Nina made a shushing sound with her mouth. Up and down she bobbed, tickling her windy fingers into the ribs of the crow and then those of her Great-grandfather.

Gray Eyes slid an empty pot onto his lap and began tapping a steady one-two beat. Closing his eyes he began a high pitched chant in the Ojibwe language. The three lost themselves in their dancing and chanting, there in the little cabin, there in the maple grove, there in the northern forest around the fire. There were no schools, no Phoebes, no roosters, no time.

Eventually they stopped and looked at one another. Gray Eyes looked happy to Eddie. It didn't show in a smile or a laugh. It was somewhere in those gray eyes. There was a light, a knowing of some kind.

"Enough," said Gray Eyes. "You need your sleep. Tomorrow we clean up and then we leave."

As Eddie slid back into his sleeping bag, he felt a sadness wash over him. The cabin, the trees, the stories of Winnebojo, the ancient smell of wood fire and the sweet scent of boiling maple sap. He was enjoying himself. But he would be leaving soon. Eddie missed his mother and father and even Leonard, the traitor. He had been missing them for some time. Tomorrow, though, he would be leaving all this for Minneapolis, and they would surely follow. The thought made him brighten just a little. He thought of seeing Kyle again, his teachers and classmates, and maybe even the long-haired girl at the skating rink.

A poke in the ribs disturbed Eddie from his thoughts. "You asleep yet?" Nina signed to her brother in the dim light from the stove door. Eddie looked over at Gray Eyes who had crawled into his sleeping bag with his back toward them.

Eddie shook his head no.

"I know you're going to be mad at me, but I don't want to go back to Minneapolis. I really, really miss Mom and Dad and Leonard. But I don't want you to go either 'cause I'd really miss you too."

"Would you really miss me, or would you really, really miss me?"

"Really, really," Nina answered. "Please don't go."

"It won't be that long anyway, Nina. Mom and Dad will miss us and come home. Besides, Dad is having trouble finding a job. Maybe he can get his old job back, and everything will be the same."

Nina was quiet for a few moments. "I don't think you can ever keep things the same. It never lets you. It loses something. I think it's like a joke. At first everyone laughs when you tell it. So then you tell it over and over and nobody laughs anymore. It's not fresh. Bemidji's fresh."

"I hate fresh," Eddie said. "I like things the way they used to be. I even like pizza better the second day. It gets better. It doesn't have to be fresh."

"I think Mom and Dad want us to have some fresh pizza," Nina said. "Besides, it's the only thing on the menu."

"So maybe we just have to go to a different restaurant," said Eddie. "Besides, you promised to go with me tomorrow. Great-grandfather promised to show us the way to get home."

Their conversation was interrupted by an owl sound coming from their Great-grandfather. "Whooo. Who-who-who-whooo. The owl is going to come and get the restless children. I can feel you fidgeting through the floorboards." Both Nina and Eddie slid deeper into their sleeping bags and fell asleep.

Chapter 19

The morning broke bright and chilly. Eddie pulled on his socks to cross the floor that had become cold during the night. He found a place to look through the window where the frost had not completely covered the pane. Little snow now remained in the clearing where the sun had shone the brightest. A thick coat of glistening frost covered the open ground except where the fire still smoldered.

After a quiet breakfast of French toast, covered with a thick layer of their own maple syrup, the trio stepped outside to break camp. The fire was stirred, the kettle scraped and scoured and rolled back to its tiny shed. The syrup, in one gallon jugs, was loaded onto the toboggan at the edge of the woods where there was still snow. The other supplies—the buckets, gunny sacks, and water jugs—were tied on the toboggan around the new syrup and sugar. When all the chores were completed, Gray Eyes looked around the camp for a last look. "It's been a good spring. I haven't been back here for a long time. Yes, this is the best spring in years."

"Except, for one thing," said Nina. "The geese, the last sign of spring. We have the maple sugar, but we haven't heard the geese yet."

"You are right," said Gray Eyes searching the skies. "It should be soon. They are due back soon."

"What do they sound like, Great-grandfather? Do they really honk?" asked Nina.

Gray Eyes looked surprised. "You've never heard wild geese?"

Nina and Eddie shook their heads.

Pulling the toboggan's long loop of rope around his waist, the old man said, "Here, each of you take one side of the rope and help. I'll try to describe the sound of the returning geese."

"People call it a honking sound. It sounds more raspy than that. It sounds more like the word 'hark'. And it carries the same meaning. Wait 'til you hear the clamoring commotion they make heading back to their favorite slough or lake in hopes that they'll find some open water. It sounds like they're proclaiming, 'Hark! We're back and we've brought the spring with us!'"

The old man's pale eyes searched the skies for signs of the Canadian geese, but seeing none, he leaned forward against the rope. Through the woods they pulled, keeping to the snowier areas so the toboggan could slide more easily. On the uphill side they all groaned against the weight and on the down hill side they all struggled to keep the toboggan from racing away.

141

After an hour, the trio stopped to rest and drink some water. "How much further do we have?" Eddie asked.

Gray Eyes didn't hear the question. Waving his hand to get the man's attention, Eddie asked the question in Gray Eye's sign language. He used the sign for distance and the sign for question.

"Another half hour," replied Gray Eyes without looking at Eddie. "Then you'll be on your way home."

Eddie felt hollow. The determination to head back to Minneapolis was fading a little. He thought of his mother and father and Leonard. Eddie wasn't sure what he should say to them when he saw them. He knew he'd like to tell them all about his adventure in the forest, and how he'd made maple sugar and the nights in the cabin and his new name and the stories he'd heard about Winnebojo.

A saying of Eddie's father suddenly came to his mind. He'd never understood it before, but now he was pretty sure he knew. "Be careful of what you wish for, because you just might get it." Now his wish to go back to Minneapolis was to be granted. The highway couldn't be far away, yet Eddie wasn't sure any more.

"Great-grandfather," Nina called, "are you

going to be able to pull this toboggan all by yourself?" She looked at Eddie. "We should help him get this to his house, shouldn't we?"

"It's no problem," said Gray Eyes shaking his head. "I'll stash it in the weeds next to the road and go get my truck. You children need to be going. Come. It's not much farther."

Nina took her place on the rope and looked over at her brother. Eddie saw tears begin to form in the corners of his sister's eyes. Looking away, she set her jaw and the three trudged forward through the last stretch of forest.

Eddie felt himself slowing. He hardly did his share of the pulling. Though Gray Eyes once looked back at Eddie, nothing was said. Eddie looked over at Nina's troubled face. She feels the same way, he thought. He tried to muster up some of the good feelings about Minneapolis—Kyle, school, the girl at the skating rink. It didn't help. Soon Eddie saw a break in the trees ahead. There seemed to be a clearing. It doesn't look like a road, Eddie thought to himself. Gray Eyes bore on toward the clearing.

Then Eddie saw it. The chicken coop. Halting in his tracks, Eddie held onto the rope forcing the toboggan to a stop. "Why did you bring us here?" Eddie cried.

"I told you I would help you get home,"

143

Gray Eyes said calmly.

"I meant home to Minneapolis. To the highway. You knew what I meant!" accused Eddie.

Holding his chin high, Gray Eyes stated, "My idea of home is not the same. My people lived in four different places every year. One for each season. Home is not your house—a pile of boards nailed together. Home is where your people are."

"I didn't want to be here. That's why we ran off."

"This family has a history of running away. Your father ran away to the city. Your grand-father ran away to the Marines. I ran away to South Dakota. We all come back after a while. Perhaps it's time to break the pattern." Gray Eyes looked off toward the house.

Eddie was confused. In one way he was relieved not to be at the highway, yet he was hurt and angry because he felt tricked.

"What about you, Great-grandfather? You're running away just as much as I am." Gray Eyes looked over at Eddie. "You can hardly hear anything, and you're too stubborn to get a hearing aid. I heard them all talking in the kitchen. They say you hardly talk to anyone or see your friends. You sit by yourself out there on the reservation.

144

Isn't that running off?"

"I get by," said Gray Eyes indignantly.

"Yeah, by yourself. And I'm hoarse from talking so loud at you. It's nobody's fault you can't hear so well, but if you can make it better . . . "

A faint noise caught Eddie's attention. He didn't know what it was at first. As it grew louder Eddie heard the high pitched honking. Geese! Eddie threw his head back and searched the sky above the tree tops. Hark, hark, hark! they seemed to cry. Suddenly, they burst into view above him, pumping their huge wings and making a terrific racket.

Eddie looked up at Gray Eyes for his reaction. There was none. Gray Eyes hadn't heard them and seemed puzzled as to what had happened to their conversation. The boy pointed up to the flock of Canadian Honkers—a magnificent V formation of black necks against an azure spring sky.

The old man stared up past the evergreen canopy for several moments after the geese were out of sight. "I never heard them," he muttered to himself. He looked down at the ground as if in thought.

Suddenly, Gray Eyes dropped the rope of the toboggan and walked out into the clearing.

Gray Eyes crossed the yard, never stopping at the house, and climbed into his pick-up. The surprised children watched the pickup chug down the driveway and disappear down the road past some khaki-colored spruce trees.

"You going in the house?" Nina asked Eddie sheepishly.

Eddie looked over at the road, now just a few steps away. He could follow the road this time and avoid the forest. He missed his family. He missed his friends and school. If they could just all be together like it was. Maybe Nina was right. Things can't always stay the same. Maybe Gray Eyes was right about the LaVoi men and their running away. But maybe his dad was running away from Minneapolis. Eddie was sure they'd come after him in Minneapolis. Eddie was frozen in his thoughts, unable to decide or move.

After a moment Eddie asked Nina, "I thought you were going to follow me?"

"I was, Eddie. Please don't be mad. I really tried, but I'm going in the house."

Something caught his attention in the tree tops. He thought he saw a large crow fly into the top of one of the pines. Goose bumps formed on Eddie's arms, and the hair on the back of his neck stood up. The crow, he thought. The crow had made one his signs to Gray Eyes. Eddie knew what he would do.

Sternly, Eddie turned toward Nina. "Little sister you are going to follow me. You're going to follow me . . . right into the house!" With that Eddie sprinted off toward the little house in the clearing. "The last one there has to feed the chickens!" he cried.

Nina tore after her brother. "Eddie," she yelled. "I love you!"

Chapter 20

Eight days later it rained all afternoon. It was the first real rain of the spring. This one wasn't mixed with snow or sleet. It was a warm rain—the kind that melts off the last remnants of dirty snow and stubborn ice hiding in the north shadows of trees, rocks and hills.

In spite of the rain, the LaVoi's belongings had to be loaded. Under a tarp, Grandfather's pickup held all the furniture that had been in the U-Haul during the trip up from Minneapolis.

While the rest of the family was finishing a late lunch, Eddie was outside tying some rope over the furniture. Just as he was checking the knots for the last time, Gray Eye's pick-up truck sliced through the mud and rattled up the drive.

Eddie watched Gray Eyes step out of his truck. He wore a new blue plaid shirt that set off the iron gray of his eyes. His long silver hair was not tied back, but hung loosely off his shoulder and down his back. When the old man saw the wagon and the pickup packed, a look of sadness moved across his face.

"So you're going back after all?"

Eddie shook his head. "No, Great-grandfather," he said loudly. "We're moving to a place just five miles from here."

Gray Eyes winced as if something was hurting. He reached up under his hair. "What?" he said now smiling. "You're not moving back to the big city?"

"No," said Eddie speaking louder. "Dad got a job doing some bookkeeping at the Cass Lake Bingo Casino. We'll be living nearer there. But it's not far. You'll have to visit us."

Again Gray Eyes looked pained and reached up under his hair. "Eddie, you've got to talk softer. This hearing aid hurts when you shout."

"Hearing aid?" Eddie shouted. "I mean, hearing aid?" he said more softly.

"Yes. You were right. I was running away even though I wasn't going anywhere. After the geese flew by and I didn't hear them, I knew I was missing too much. I had decided I was too old. After you said those things to me, I decided you were right. I've since decided that I'll be alive until I'm not. I went to the hearing clinic and they did some tests, and this is what they ordered for me. It's taking some getting used to." Gray Eyes lifted his hair and turned so Eddie could see the aid.

Eddie hopped down from the box of the truck. "You know everybody was worried about you. You left all that maple sugar and syrup and

149

all your stuff. You wouldn't answer your phone. We called your neighbor to check up on you and she said you looked fine, but you were just sitting there in your house."

"I was thinking."

"Yeah," Eddie added, "I've been doing a lot of thinking too. And I want to thank you. Thank-you for saving us from the blizzard and for the spring mapling and for the stories. Mostly, I think you saved me from a big mistake."

Gray Eyes nodded. "I need to thank you too. I taught you some of the old ways, but you taught me that new isn't all bad. Also, you taught me avoiding people is running away. This family has had enough of that."

Eddie stepped forward and hugged his great-grandfather. Then Eddie said, "I have one more sign I want to show you from my sign language. Watch!" Cupping his right hand near his face, Eddie touched his fingertips to the lower part of his cheek and then moved them to the upper cheek."

Gray Eyes looked surprised. "That's the sign the crow made in my dream the night before I gave you your name."

Eddie swallowed hard. "It means home. That's my sign for home. Great-grandfather, you couldn't have known that sign, even though it was in your dream. I knew what the sign meant right away when you described the crow's wings."

The pair stood for a moment in amazement.

"Let's go inside," said Gray Eyes. "Our people are in there."

Eddie proudly walked alongside Gray Eyes toward the house. On the top step, Gray Eyes suddenly spun around. Looking up at the tree tops he softly said, "They're coming."

Then Eddie heard them. Squinting up into the clearing clouds, Eddie and Gray Eyes together beheld the clamor of honking and harking and a black blur of long thin necks with white cheek patches. It was all accompanied by the powerful, slashing of gray wings against the wet buoyancy of the spring air. Eddie and Gray Eyes watched transfixed as the geese knifed through the sky above them and carried the arrival of spring and rebirth on their tailfeathers.

ABOUT THE AUTHOR

Patrick J. Quinn, in addition to writing and illustrating books for young people, is a communication disorders specialist, who works with middle-school aged students in New Prague, Minnesota. Patrick lives in Prior Lake, Minnesota with his family and enjoys playing guitar and mandolin in a musical group, biking and, of course, reading.

Also available by Patrick Quinn
for the Young Adult Reader

Matthew Pinkowski's
Special Summer

In his own wry, wonderful words, thirteen-year-old Matthew
Pinkowski shares the summer of his life. Matthew always enjoyed summer more than most kids because of his trouble with reading and writing. But this summer starts with a bang in his new hometown, Stillwater,
Minnesota, when his quick thinking helps save a neighborhood kid in a
runaway car. Matthew meets the car's passenger, Tommy, who moves
and learns slowly, but who also has his own talents; Sandy, Tommy's
sister and an acrobatic girl with her own opinions; and Laura, a deaf girl
visiting her overly protective aunt and uncle.

Matthew leads his new friends on one adventure after another. He
tells of discovering a secret cave above the river, and of figuring out a
tricky strategy for a poker game with local bullies. And in an ultimate,
thrilling challenge, he and his friends decide to find out who has been
stealing boats from the river marina. By summer's end, Matthew knows
to expect the best of people, including himself. His funny, true-to-life
story makes his special summer a memorable one for readers as well.

I.S.B.N. # 0-9645048-1-2 $7.95

Eagle Creek Publications
14160 Rolling Oaks Circle
Prior Lake, MN 55372

To order: send me _____ copies of **Matthew Pinkowski's
Special Summer**. I am enclosing $_____(please add $2.00 to
cover postage and handling). Send check or money order, no cash or
C.O.D.. Please allow up to 4 weeks for shipment. Prices are subject to
change without notice.

Name_____
Address_____
City_____State_____Zip_____